Pea, Bee, & Jay

GOTTA FIND GRAMPS

Brian "Smitty" Smith

HARPER alley

An Imprint of HarperCollins*Publishers*

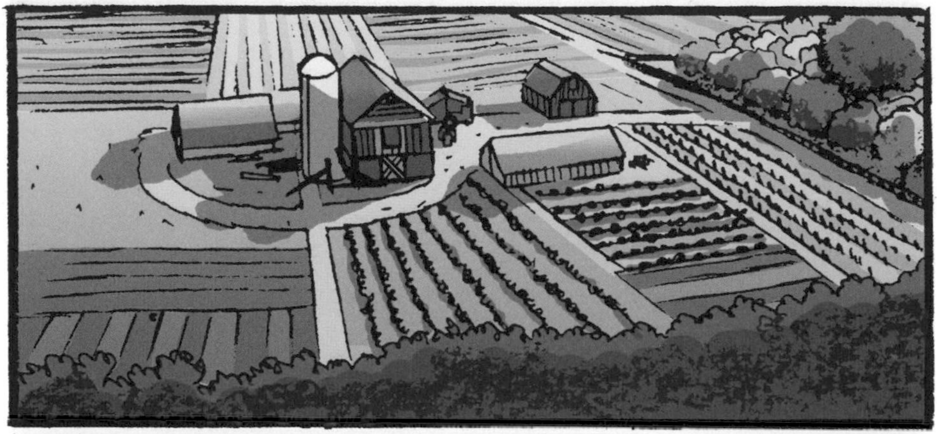

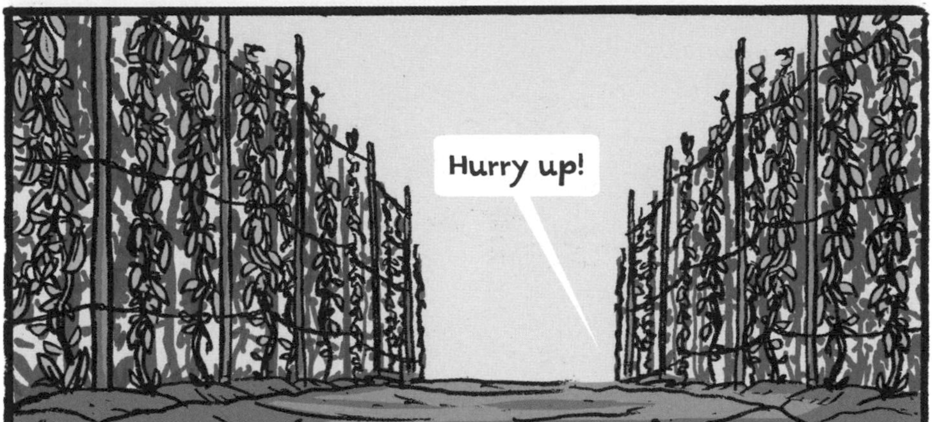
Hurry up!

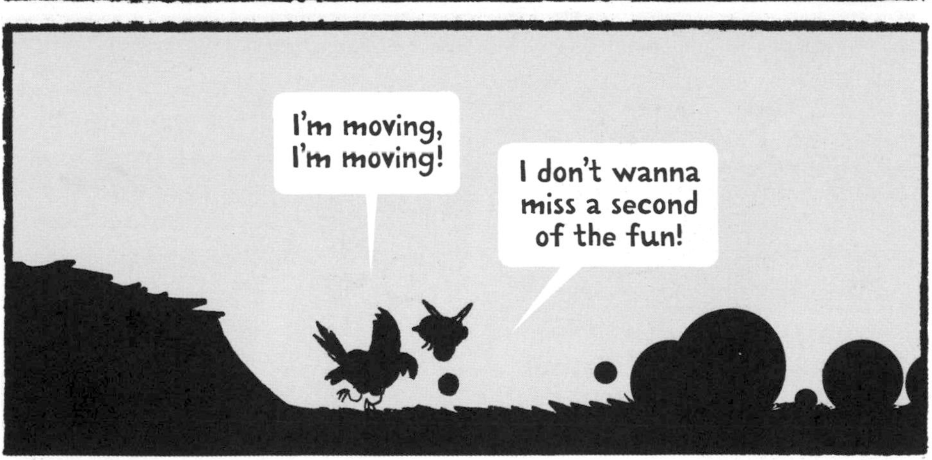
I'm moving, I'm moving!
I don't wanna miss a second of the fun!

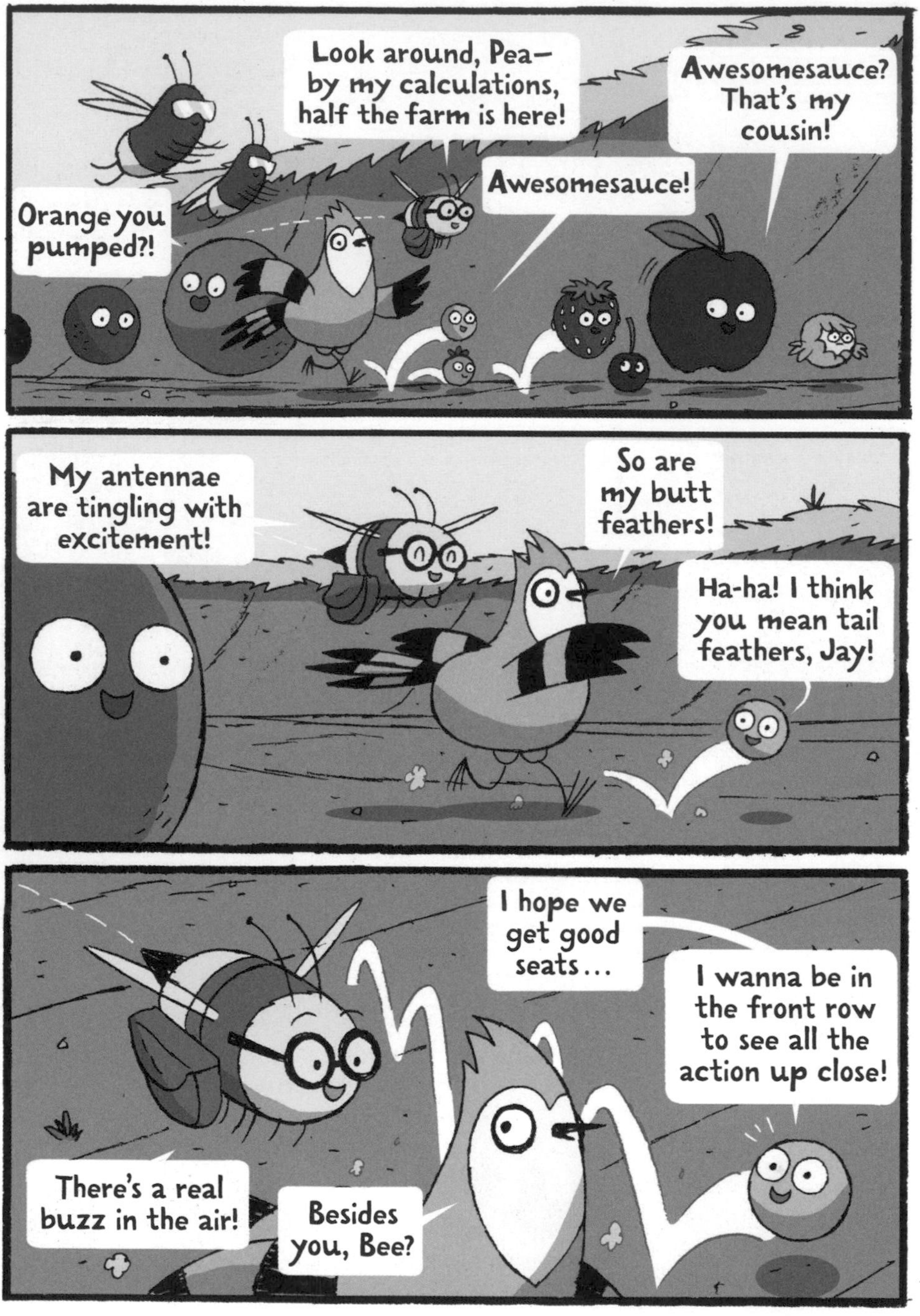

Orange you pumped?!
Look around, Pea— by my calculations, half the farm is here!
Awesomesauce!
Awesomesauce? That's my cousin!
My antennae are tingling with excitement!
So are my butt feathers!
Ha-ha! I think you mean tail feathers, Jay!
There's a real buzz in the air!
Besides you, Bee?
I hope we get good seats...
I wanna be in the front row to see all the action up close!

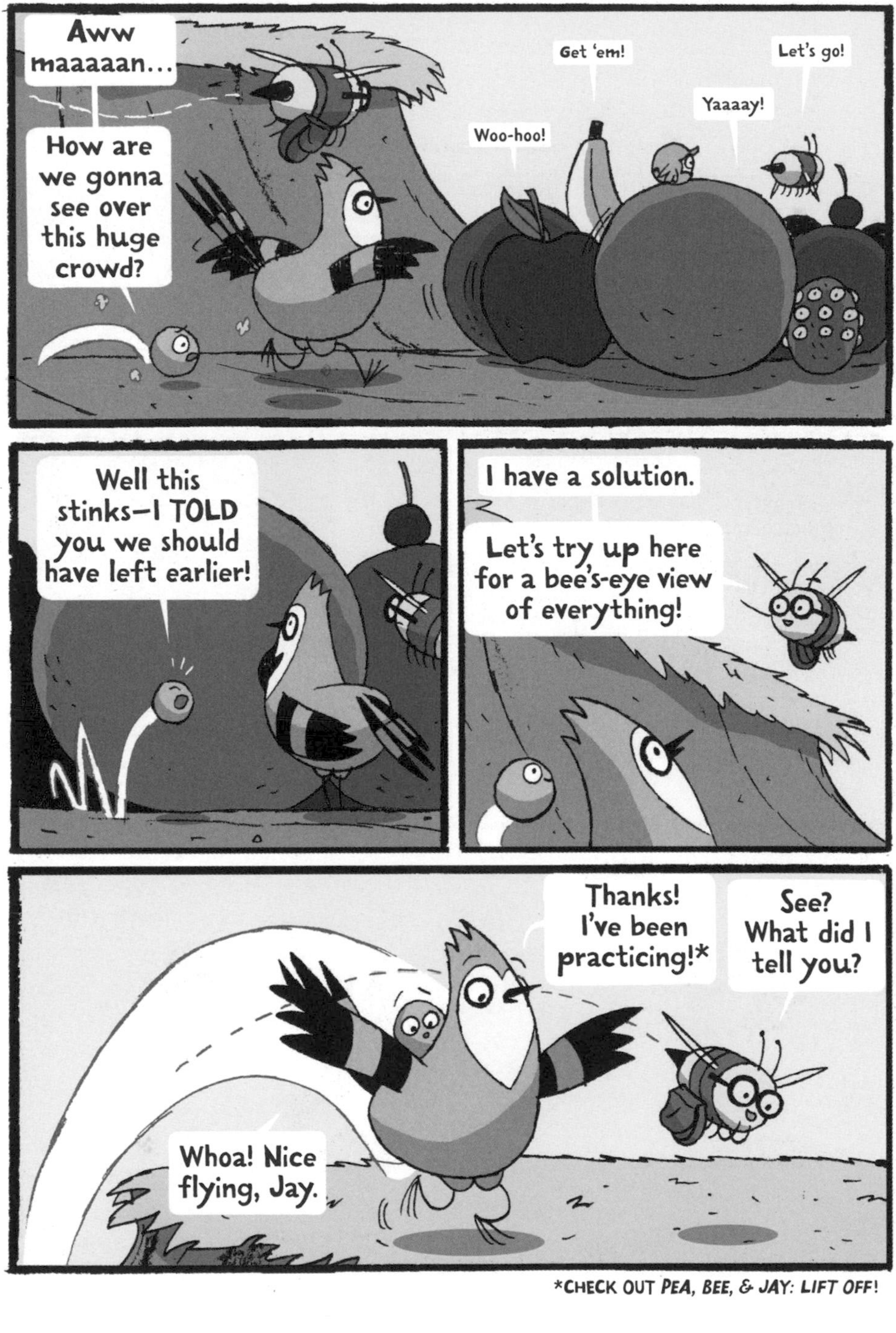
Aww maaaaan...
How are we gonna see over this huge crowd?
Woo-hoo!
Get 'em!
Yaaaay!
Let's go!
Well this stinks—I TOLD you we should have left earlier!
I have a solution.
Let's try up here for a bee's-eye view of everything!
Whoa! Nice flying, Jay.
Thanks! I've been practicing!*
See? What did I tell you?

*CHECK OUT *PEA, BEE, & JAY: LIFT OFF*!

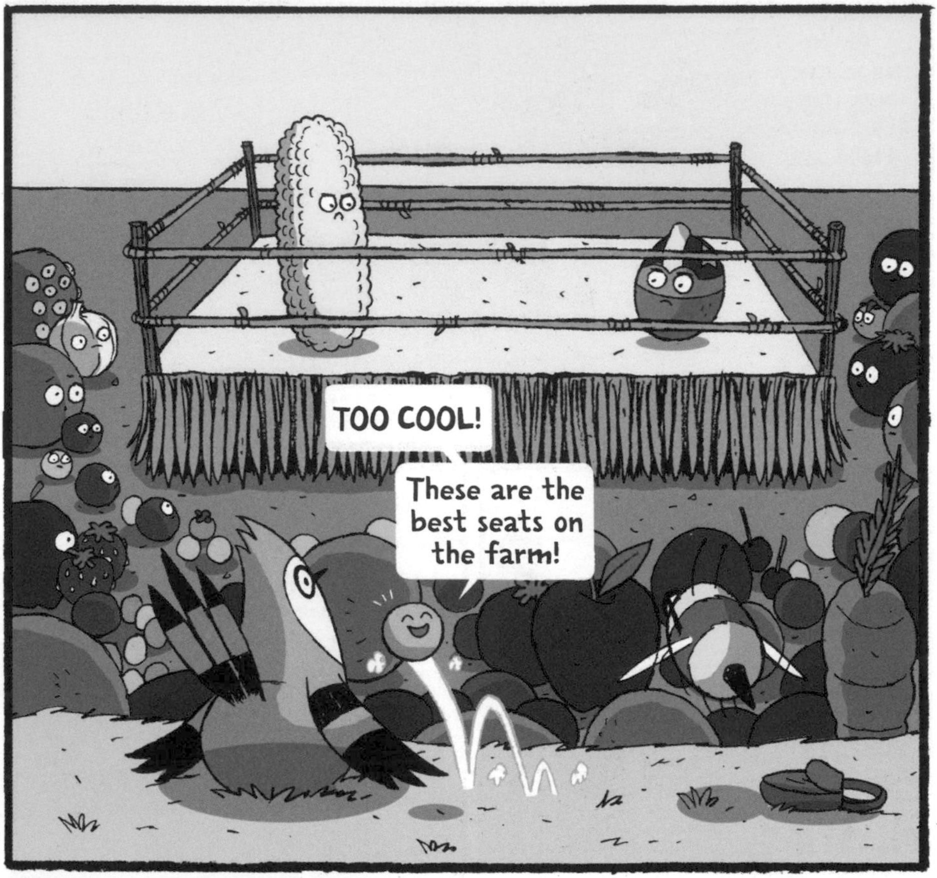
TOO COOL!
These are the best seats on the farm!

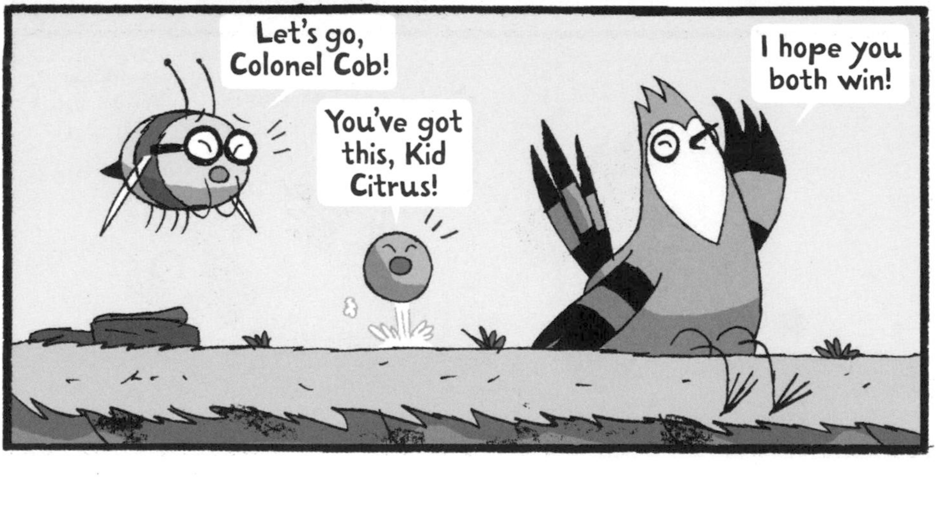
Let's go, Colonel Cob!
You've got this, Kid Citrus!
I hope you both win!

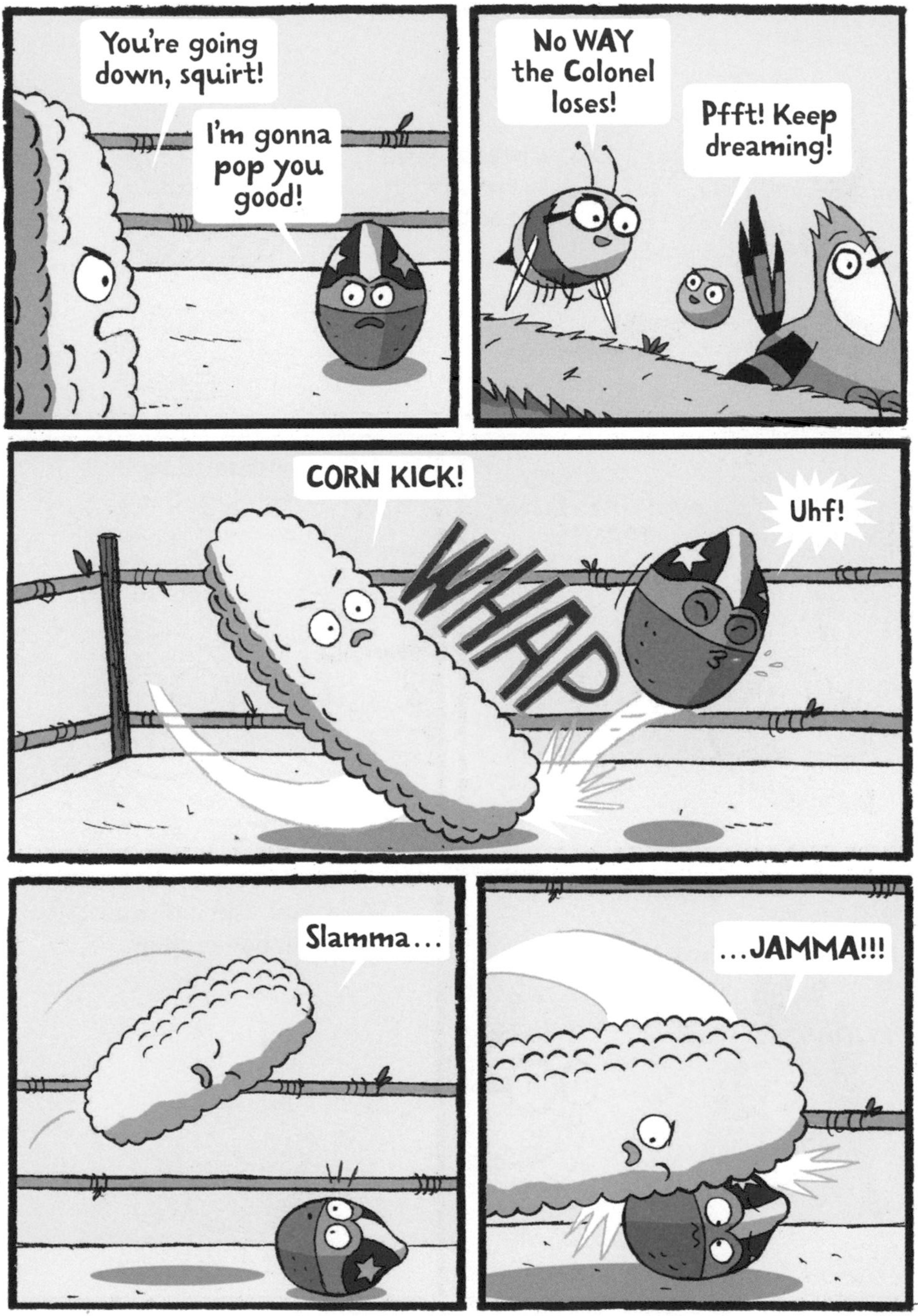
You're going down, squirt!
I'm gonna pop you good!
No WAY the Colonel loses!
Pfft! Keep dreaming!
CORN KICK!
WHAP
Uhf!
Slamma...
...JAMMA!!!

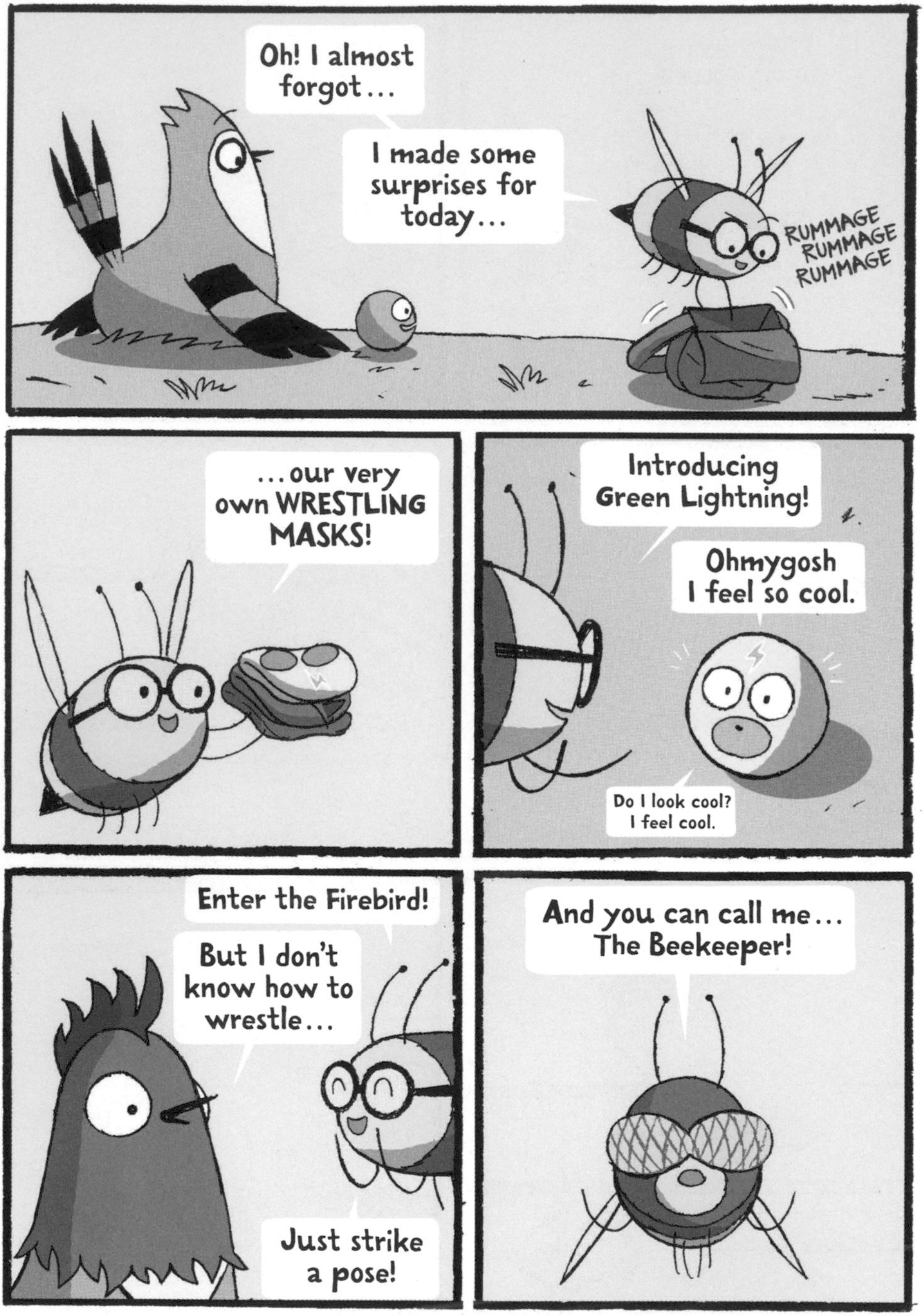
Oh! I almost forgot...
I made some surprises for today...
RUMMAGE RUMMAGE RUMMAGE
...our very own WRESTLING MASKS!
Introducing Green Lightning!
Ohmygosh I feel so cool.
Do I look cool? I feel cool.
Enter the Firebird!
But I don't know how to wrestle...
Just strike a pose!
And you can call me... The Beekeeper!

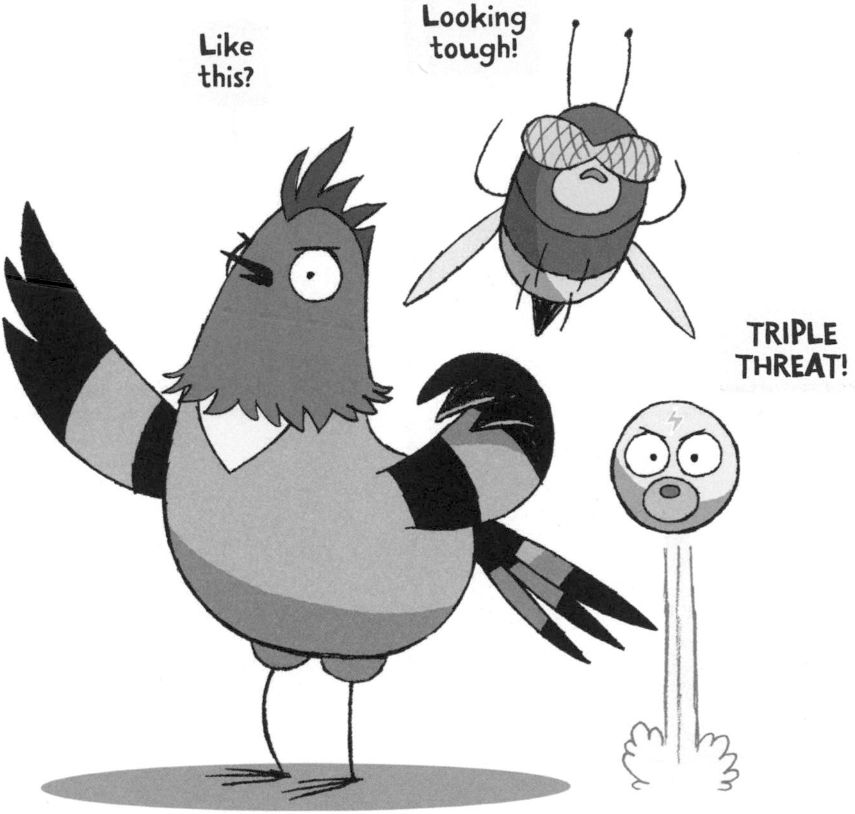
Like this?
Looking tough!
TRIPLE THREAT!

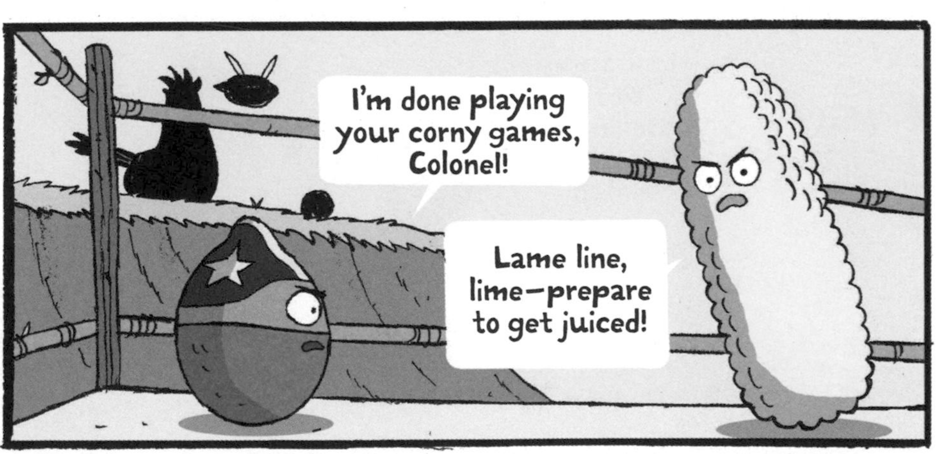
I'm done playing your corny games, Colonel!
Lame line, lime—prepare to get juiced!

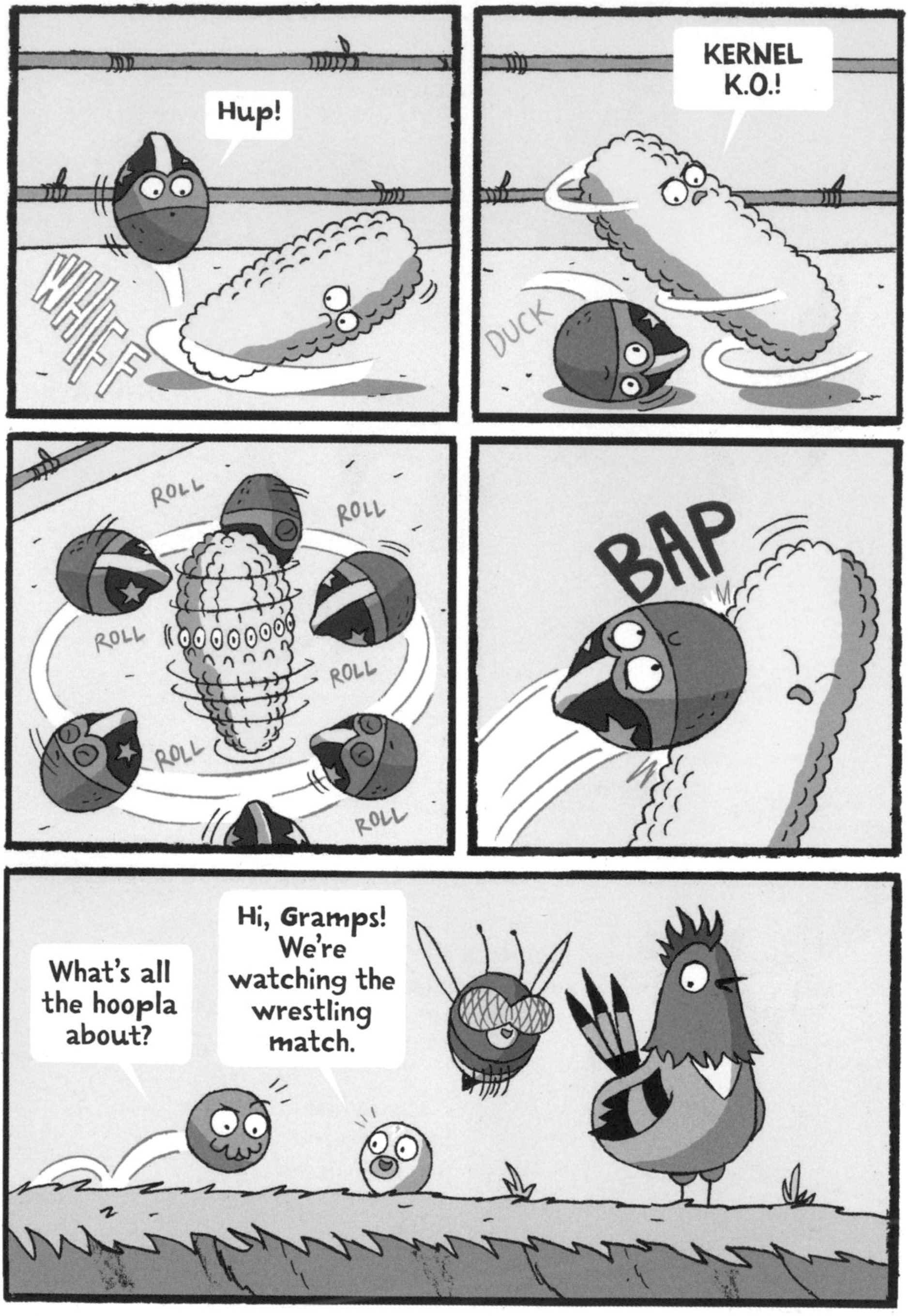
Hup!
WHIFF
KERNEL K.O.!
DUCK
ROLL
ROLL
ROLL
ROLL
ROLL
ROLL
BAP
What's all the hoopla about?
Hi, Gramps! We're watching the wrestling match.

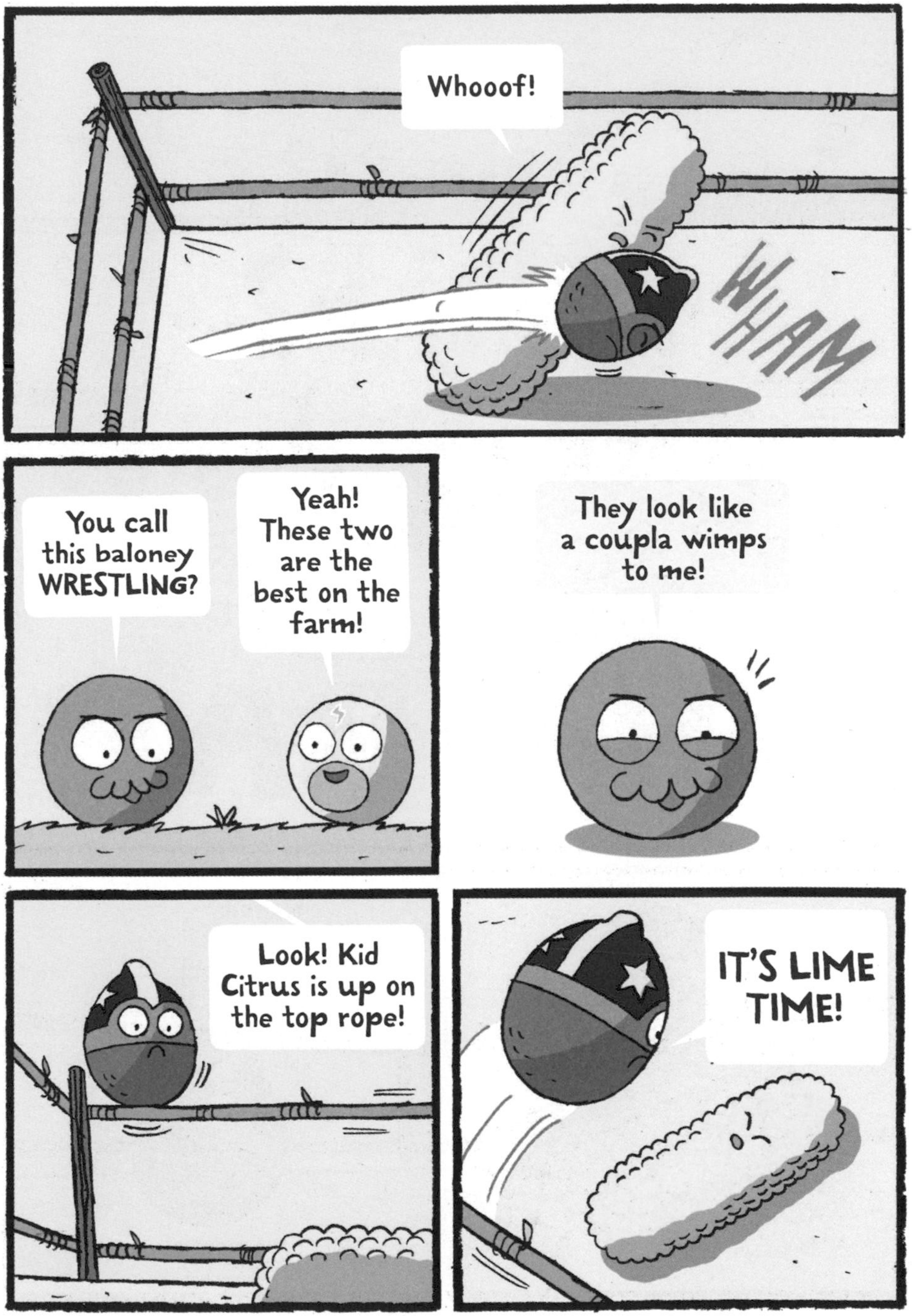
Whooof!
WHAM
You call this baloney WRESTLING?
Yeah! These two are the best on the farm!
They look like a coupla wimps to me!
Look! Kid Citrus is up on the top rope!
IT'S LIME TIME!

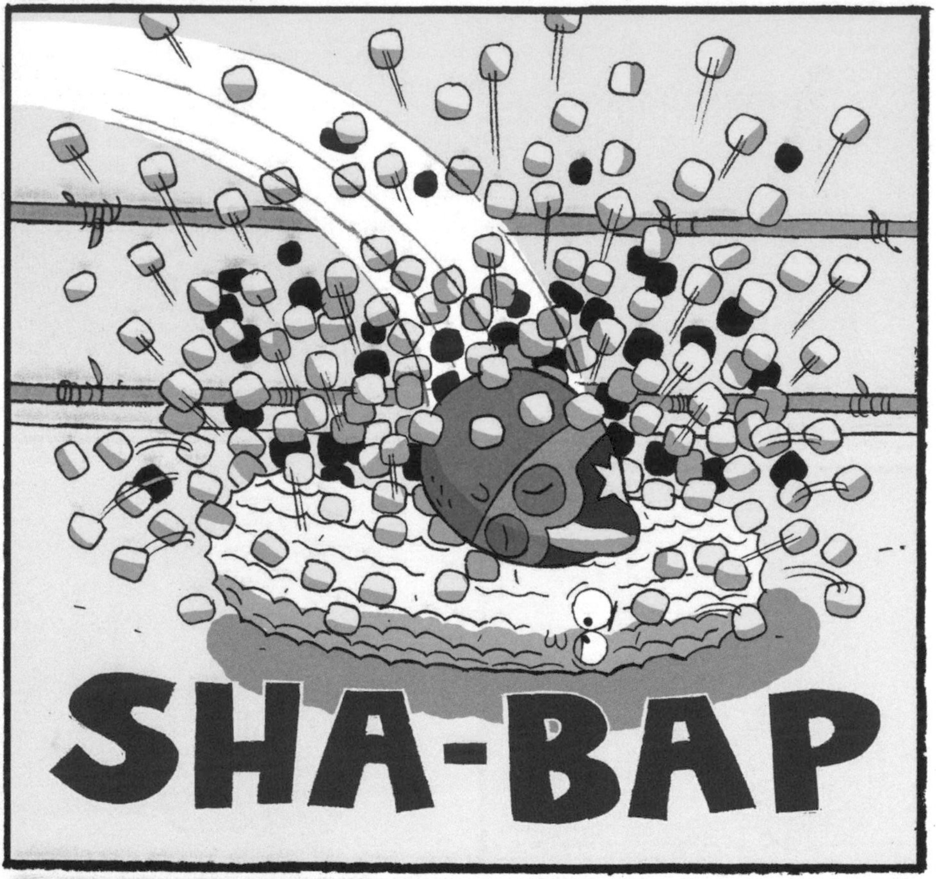
SHA-BAP

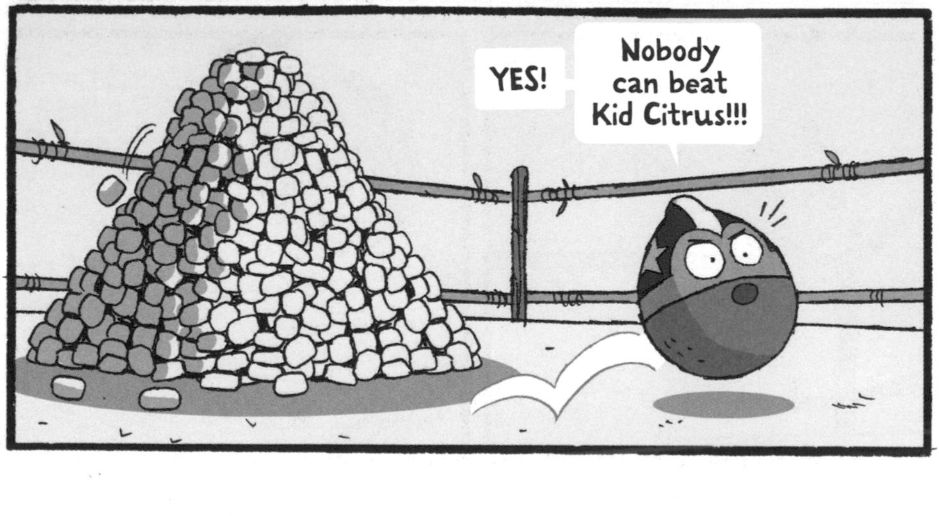
YES!
Nobody can beat Kid Citrus!!!

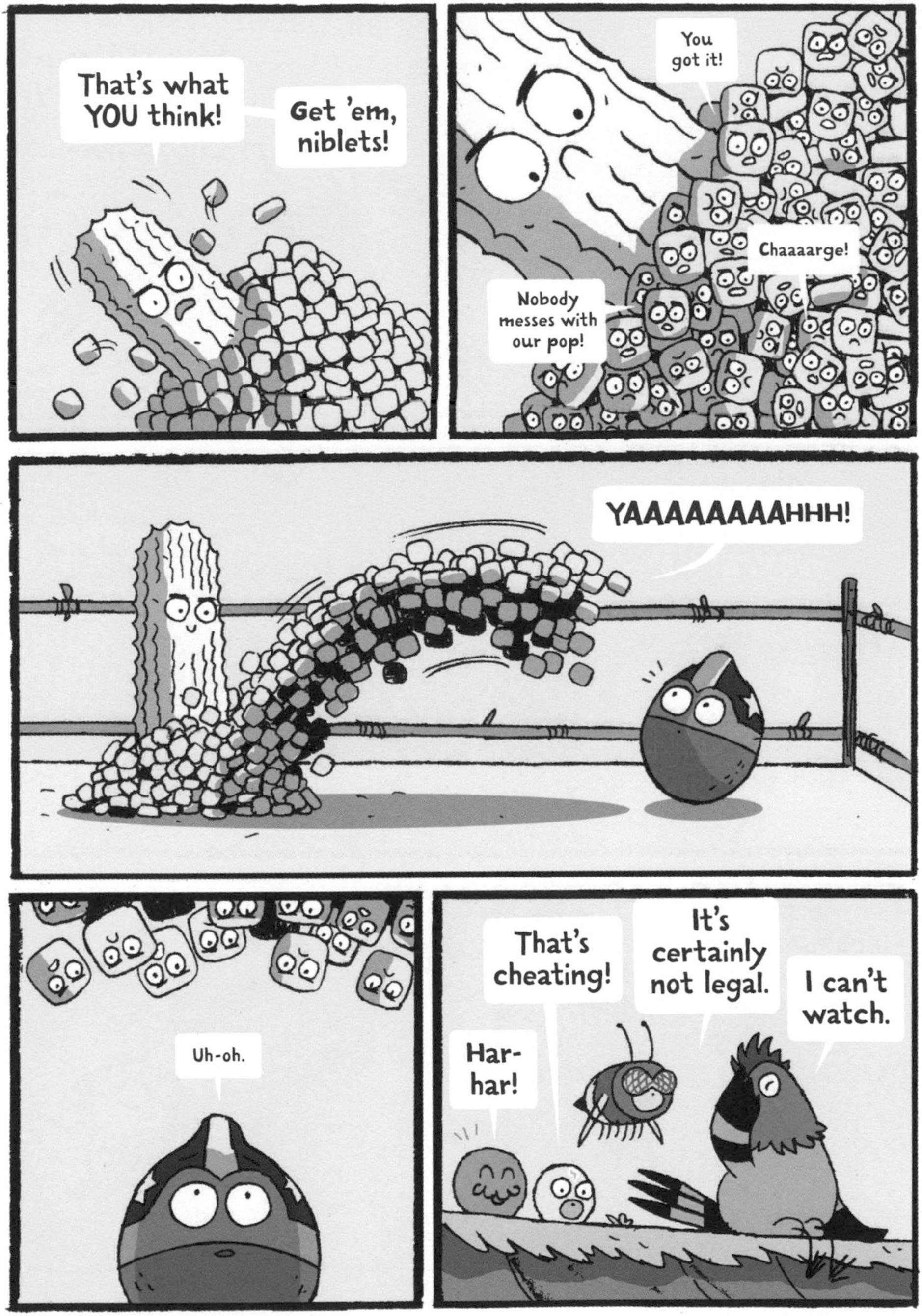

That's what YOU think!
Get 'em, niblets!
You got it!
Chaaaarge!
Nobody messes with our pop!
YAAAAAAAAHHH!
Uh-oh.
Har-har!
That's cheating!
It's certainly not legal.
I can't watch.

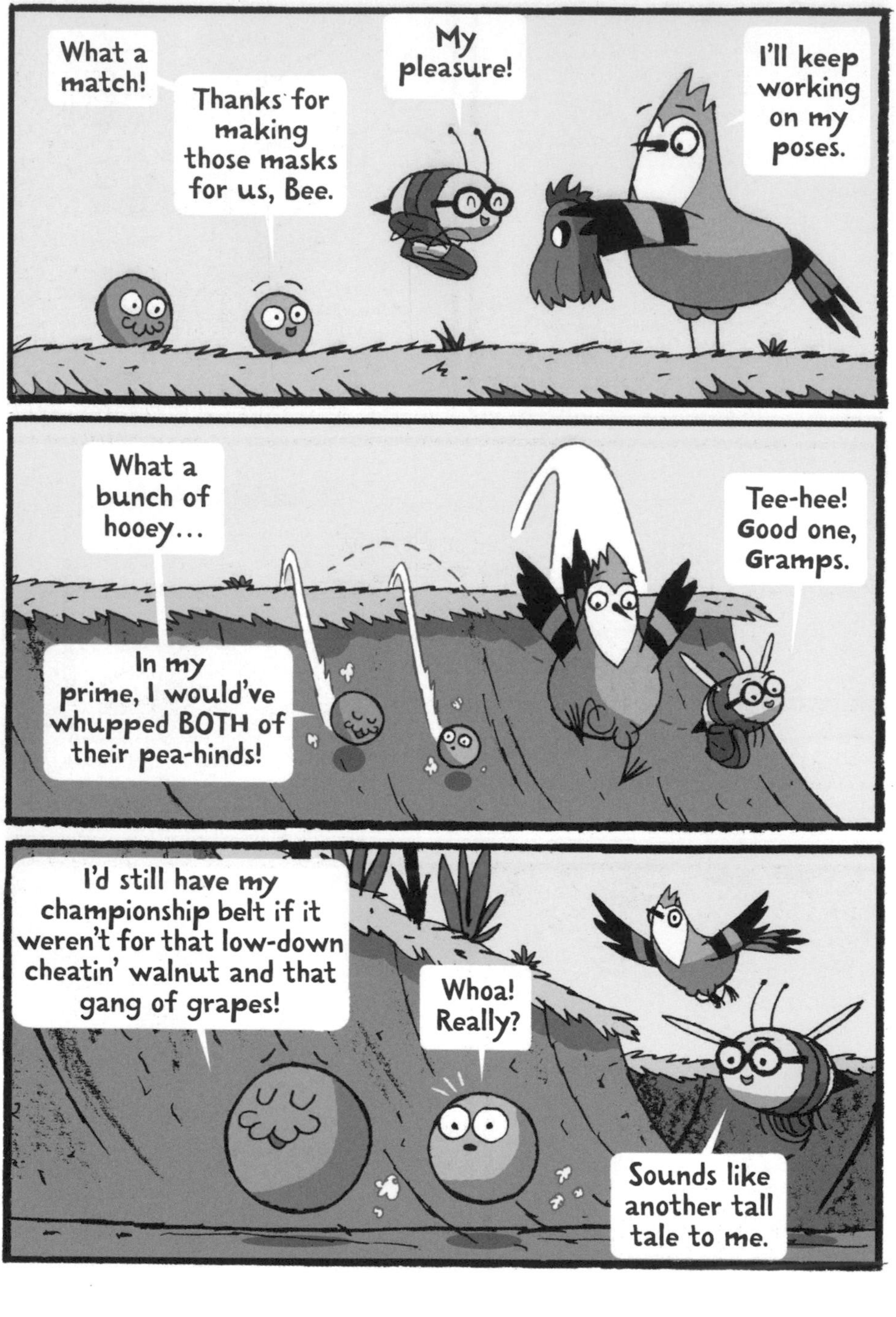
What a match!
Thanks for making those masks for us, Bee.
My pleasure!
I'll keep working on my poses.
What a bunch of hooey...
In my prime, I would've whupped BOTH of their pea-hinds!
Tee-hee! Good one, Gramps.
I'd still have my championship belt if it weren't for that low-down cheatin' walnut and that gang of grapes!
Whoa! Really?
Sounds like another tall tale to me.

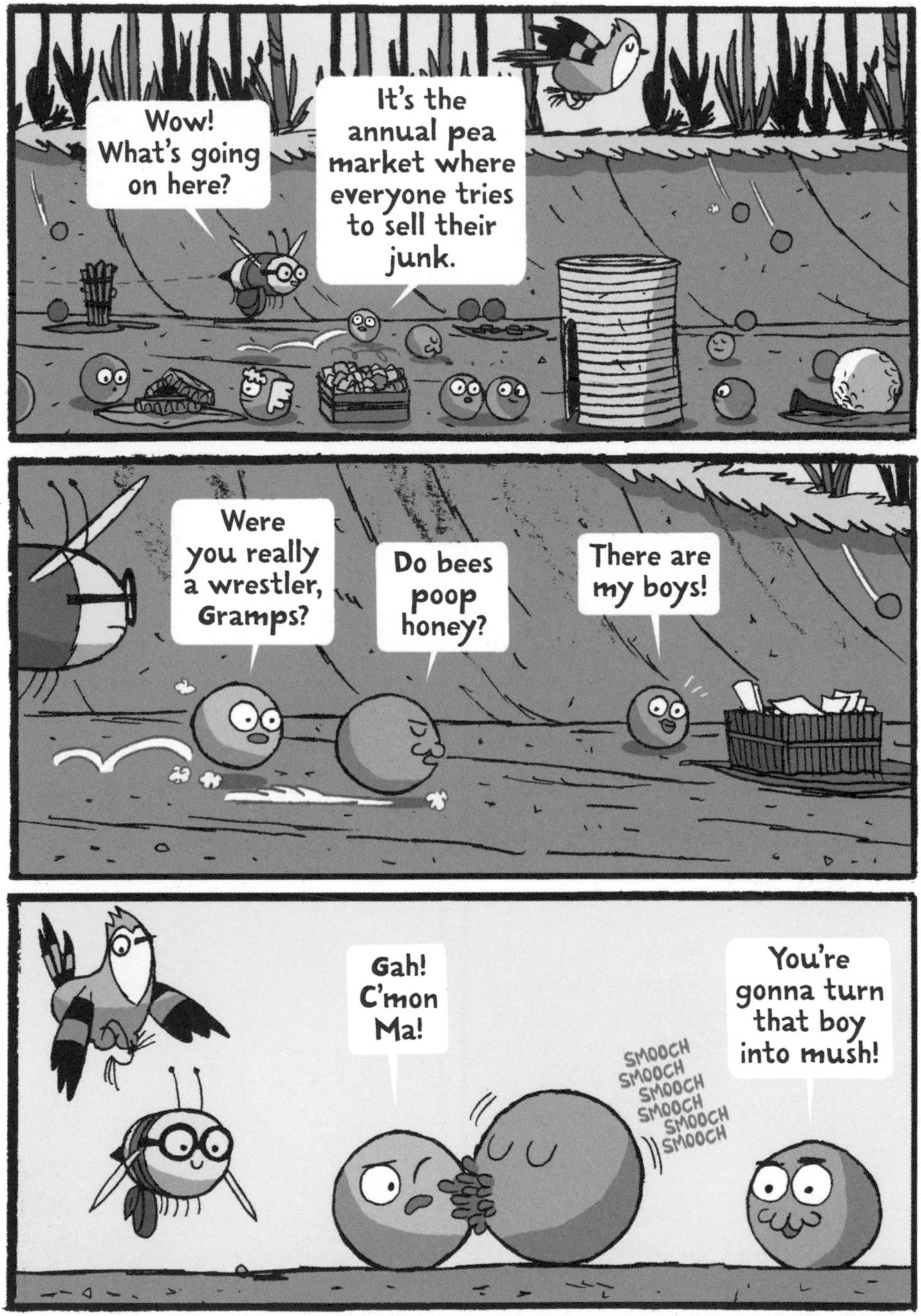
Wow! What's going on here?
It's the annual pea market where everyone tries to sell their junk.
Were you really a wrestler, Gramps?
Do bees poop honey?
There are my boys!
Gah! C'mon Ma!
SMOOCH SMOOCH SMOOCH SMOOCH SMOOCH SMOOCH
You're gonna turn that boy into mush!

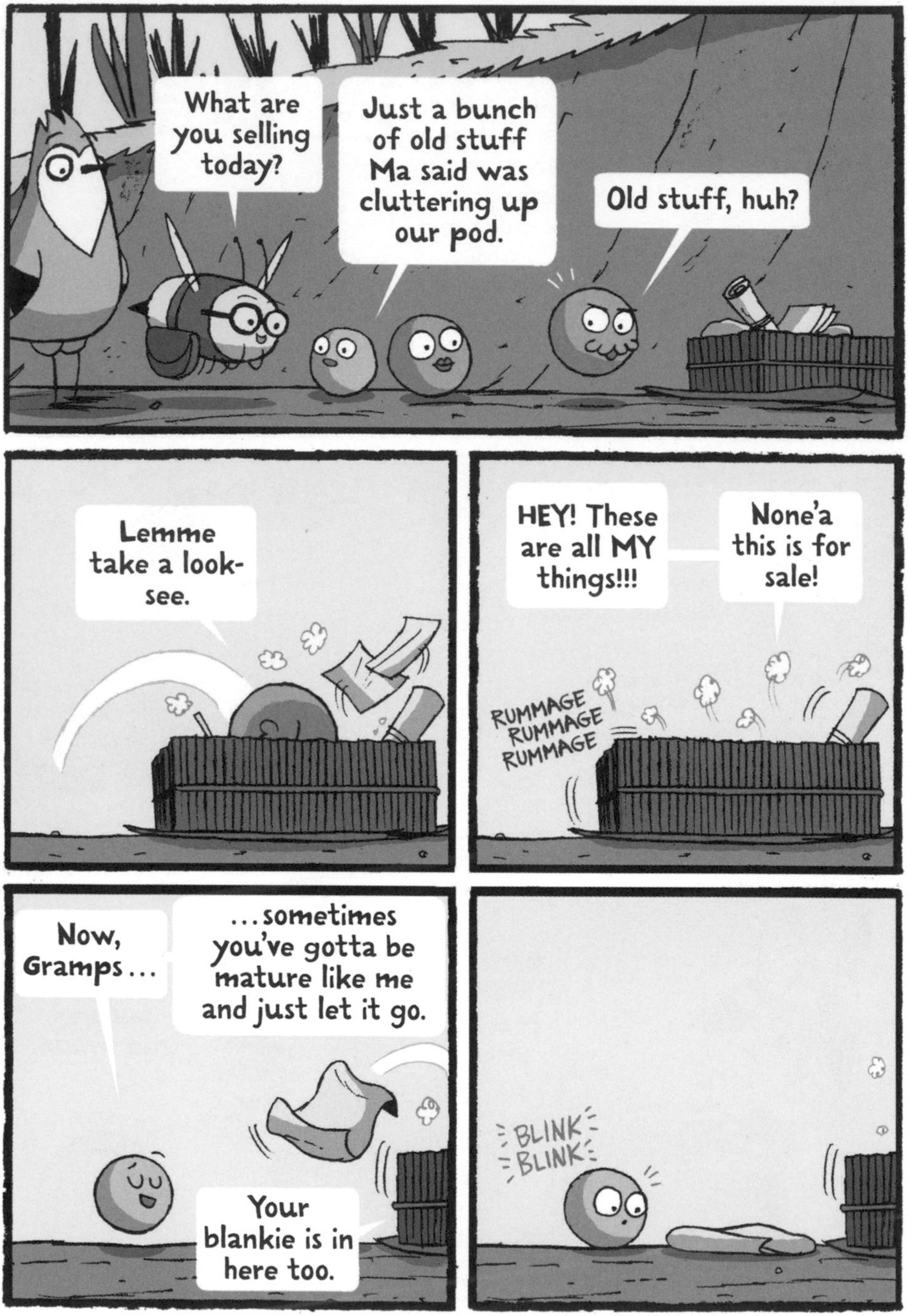
What are you selling today?
Just a bunch of old stuff Ma said was cluttering up our pod.
Old stuff, huh?
Lemme take a look-see.
HEY! These are all MY things!!!
None'a this is for sale!
RUMMAGE RUMMAGE RUMMAGE
Now, Gramps...
...sometimes you've gotta be mature like me and just let it go.
Your blankie is in here too.
BLINK BLINK

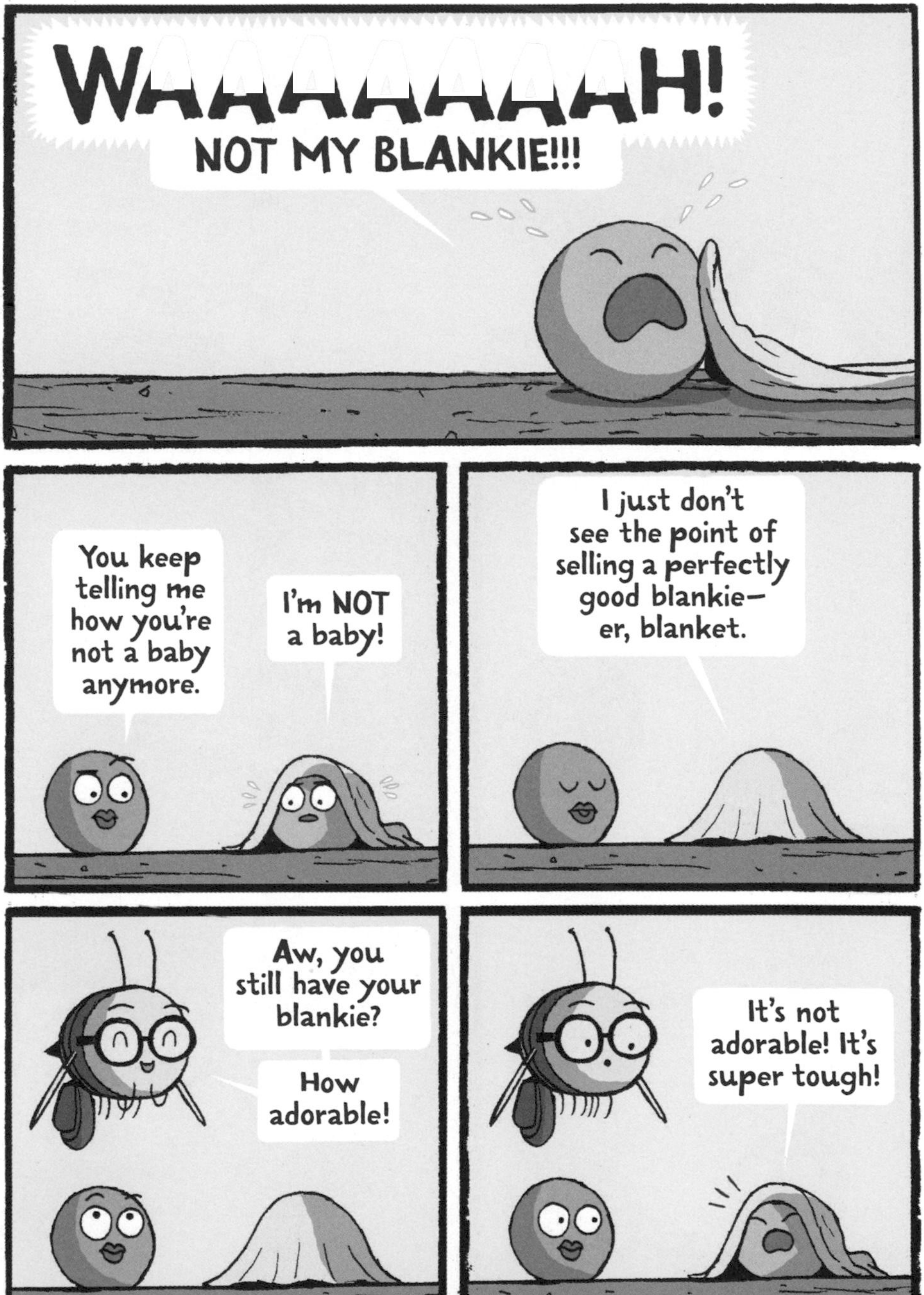
WAAAAAAAAAH!
NOT MY BLANKIE!!!
You keep telling me how you're not a baby anymore.
I'm NOT a baby!
I just don't see the point of selling a perfectly good blankie— er, blanket.
Aw, you still have your blankie?
How adorable!
It's not adorable! It's super tough!

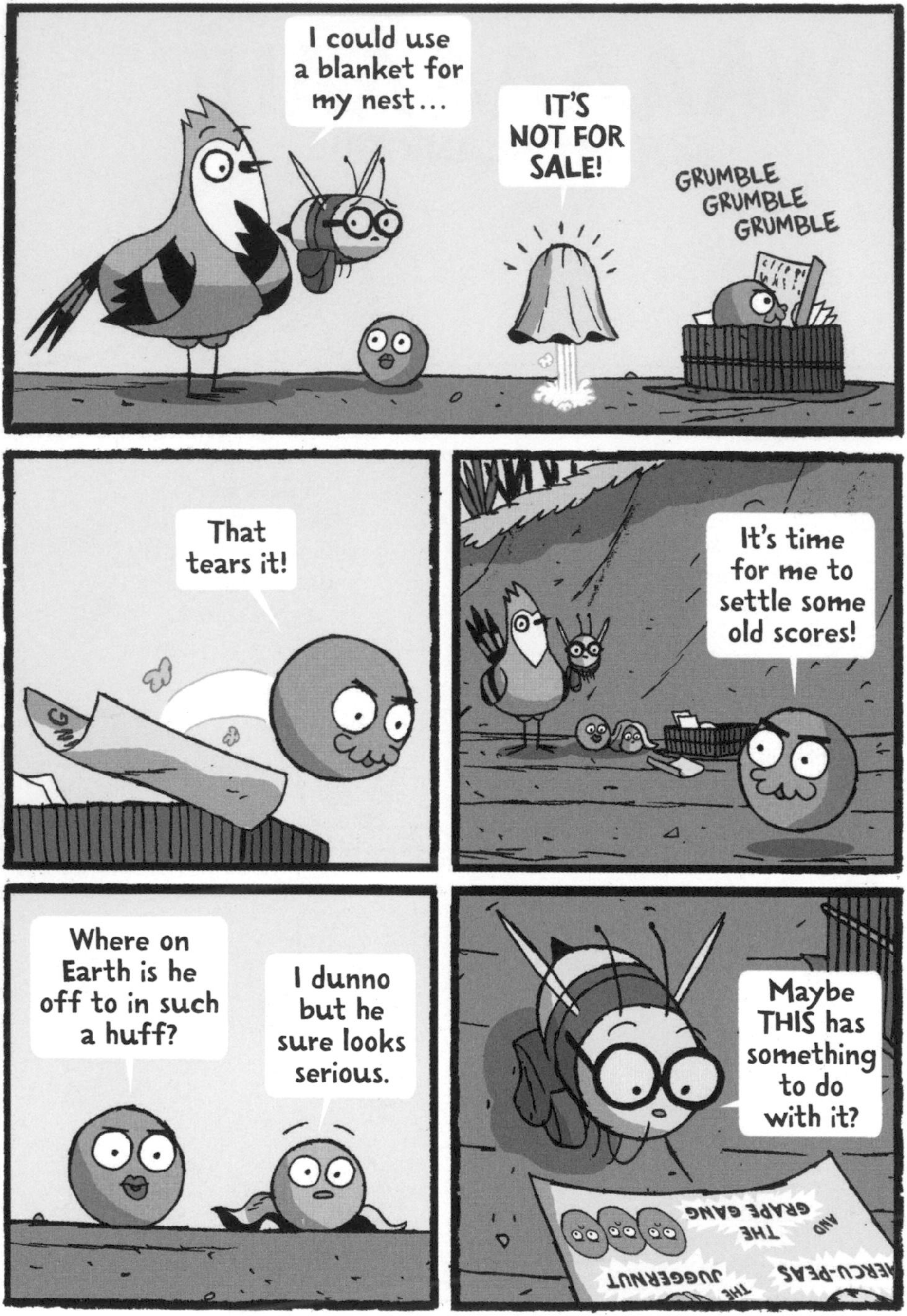

I could use a blanket for my nest...
IT'S NOT FOR SALE!
GRUMBLE GRUMBLE GRUMBLE
That tears it!
It's time for me to settle some old scores!
Where on Earth is he off to in such a huff?
I dunno but he sure looks serious.
Maybe THIS has something to do with it?
THE JUGGERNAUT
AND THE GRAPE GANG

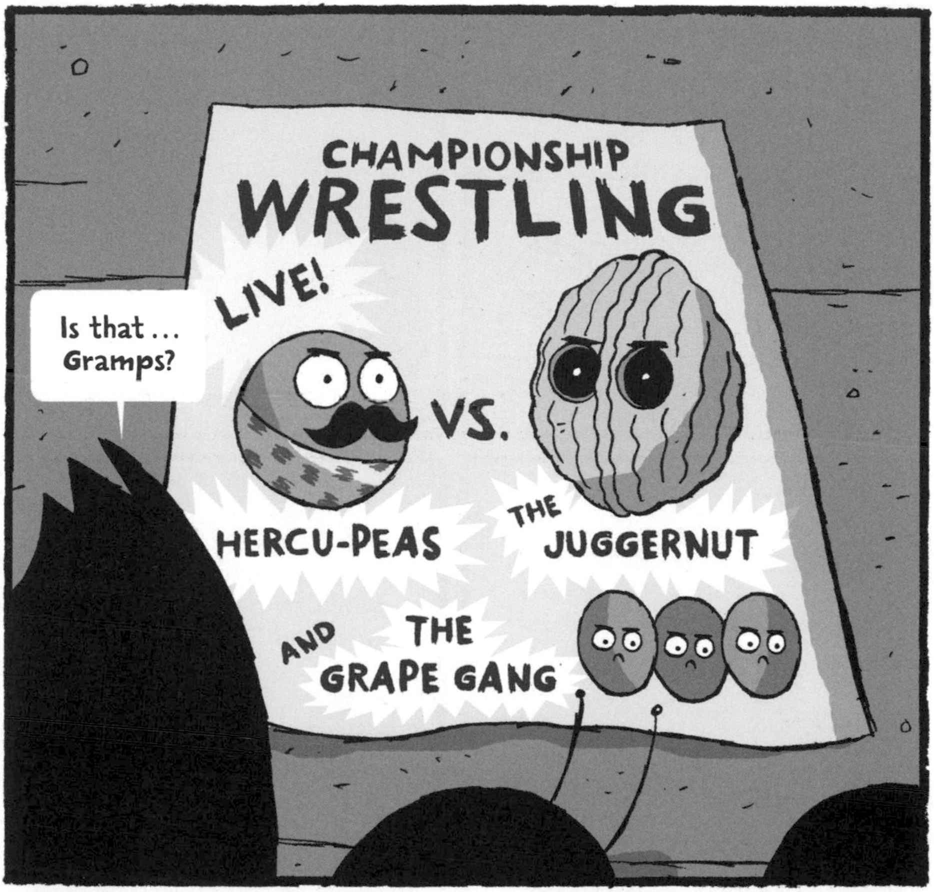
CHAMPIONSHIP WRESTLING
LIVE!
Is that ... Gramps?
VS.
HERCU-PEAS
THE JUGGERNUT
AND THE GRAPE GANG

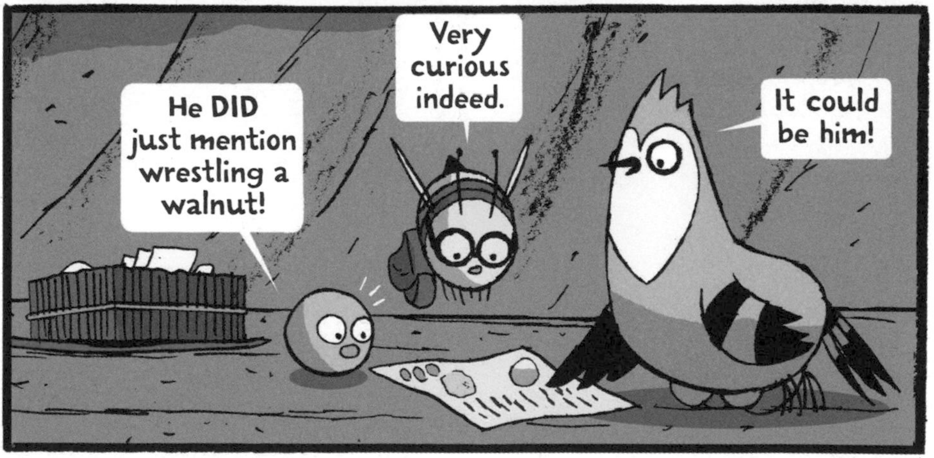
He DID just mention wrestling a walnut!
Very curious indeed.
It could be him!

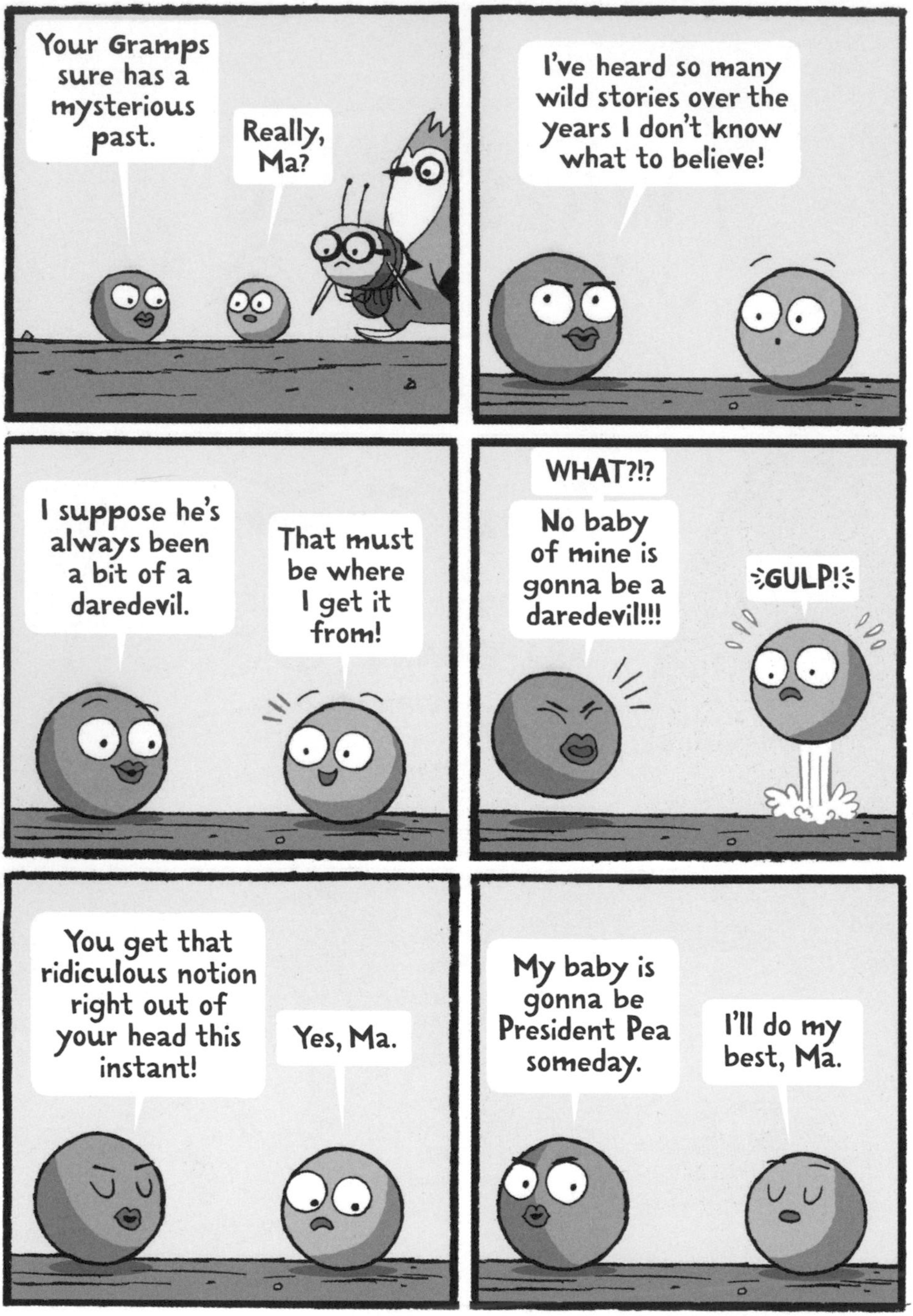

Your Gramps sure has a mysterious past.
Really, Ma?
I've heard so many wild stories over the years I don't know what to believe!
I suppose he's always been a bit of a daredevil.
That must be where I get it from!
WHAT?!?
No baby of mine is gonna be a daredevil!!!
GULP!
You get that ridiculous notion right out of your head this instant!
Yes, Ma.
My baby is gonna be President Pea someday.
I'll do my best, Ma.

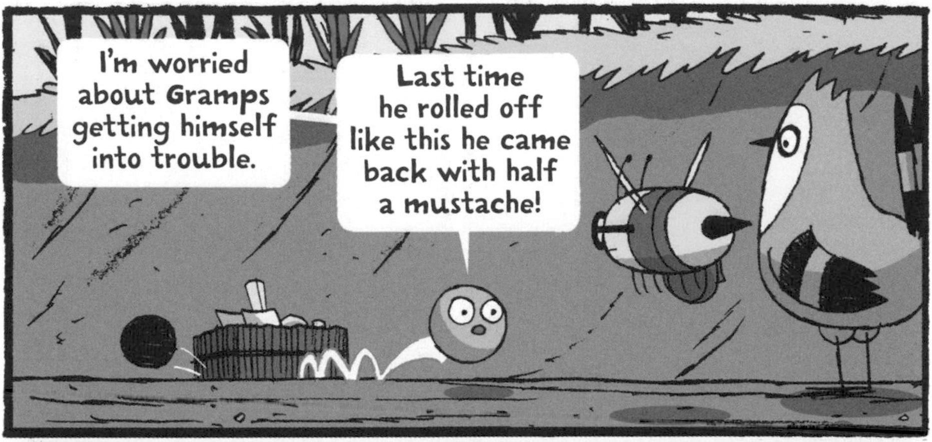
I'm worried about Gramps getting himself into trouble.
Last time he rolled off like this he came back with half a mustache!

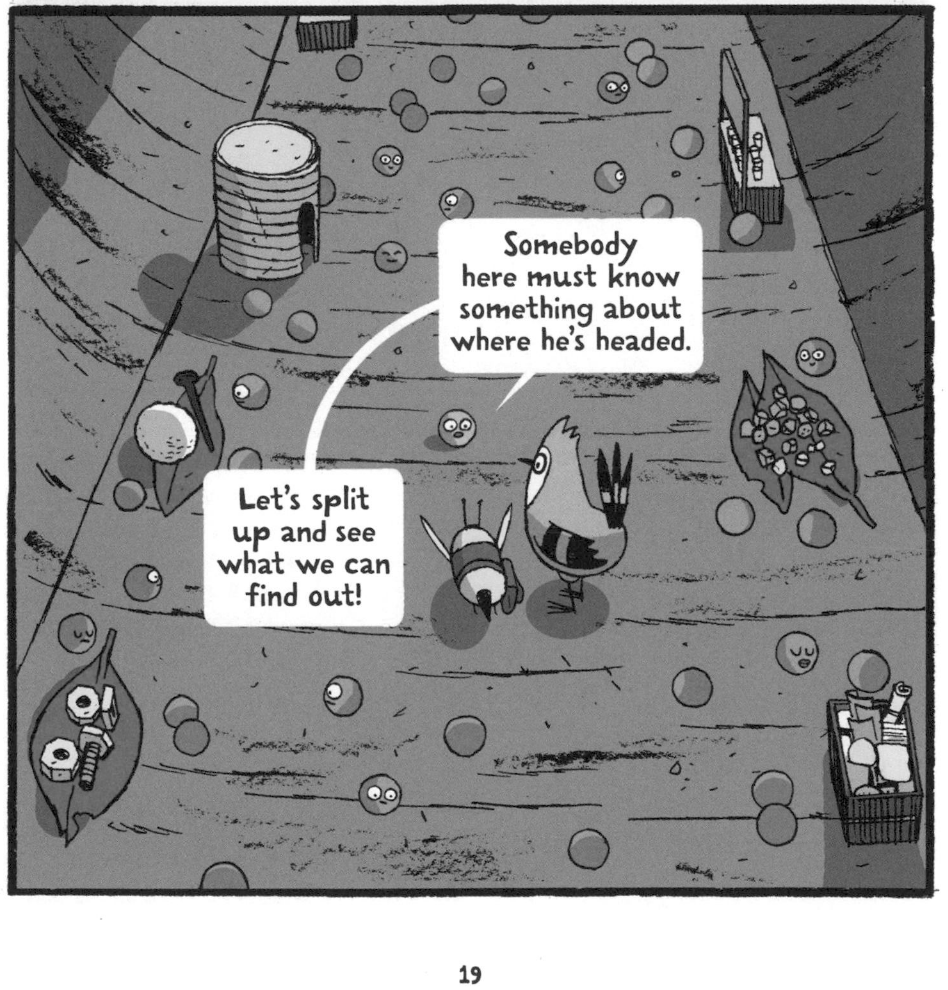
Somebody here must know something about where he's headed.
Let's split up and see what we can find out!

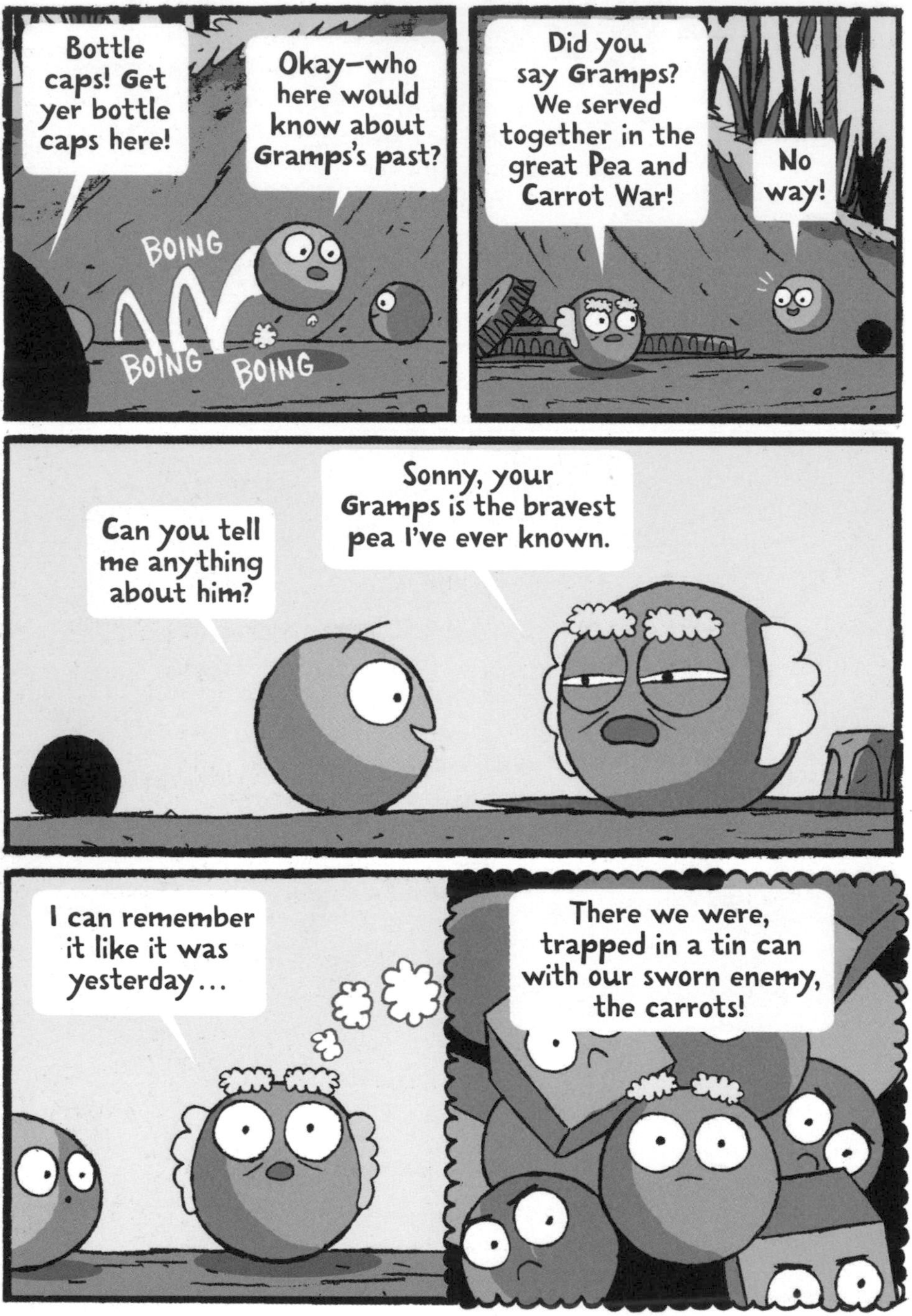

Bottle caps! Get yer bottle caps here!
Okay—who here would know about Gramps's past?
BOING
BOING
BOING
Did you say Gramps? We served together in the great Pea and Carrot War!
No way!
Can you tell me anything about him?
Sonny, your Gramps is the bravest pea I've ever known.
I can remember it like it was yesterday...
There we were, trapped in a tin can with our sworn enemy, the carrots!

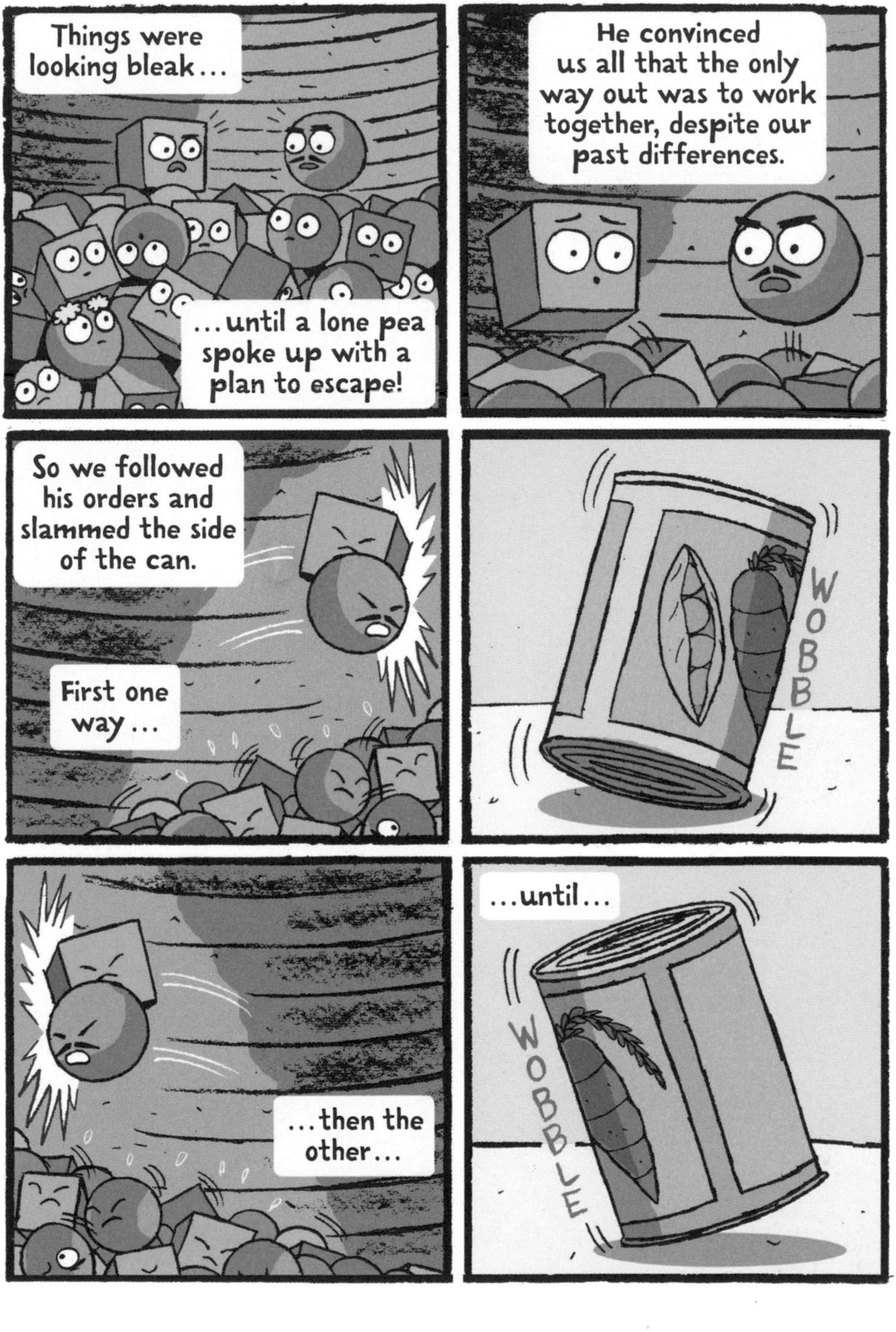

Things were looking bleak...
...until a lone pea spoke up with a plan to escape!
He convinced us all that the only way out was to work together, despite our past differences.
So we followed his orders and slammed the side of the can.
First one way...
WOBBLE
...then the other...
...until...
WOBBLE

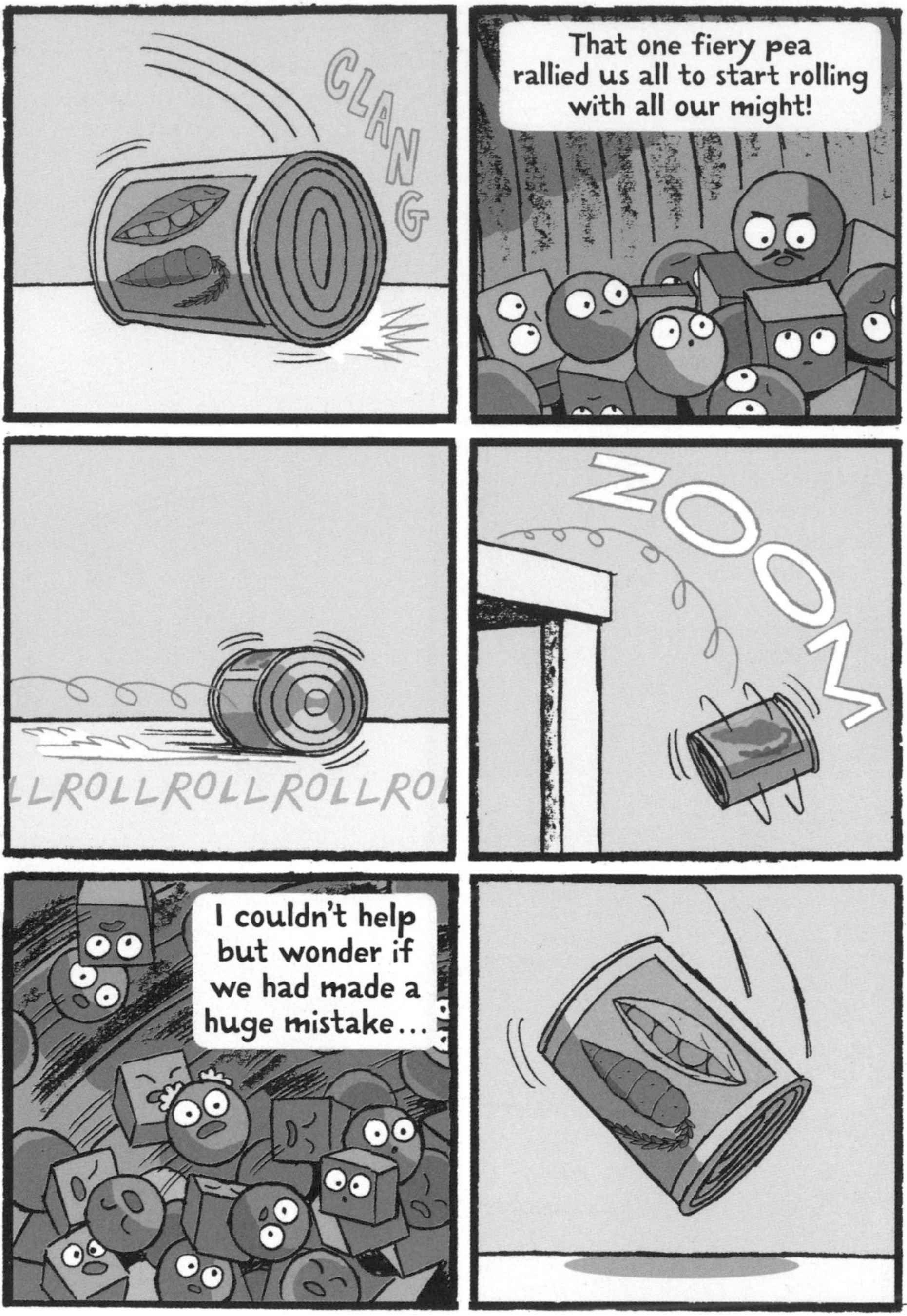
CLANG
That one fiery pea rallied us all to start rolling with all our might!
LLROLLROLLROLLRO
ZOOM
I couldn't help but wonder if we had made a huge mistake...

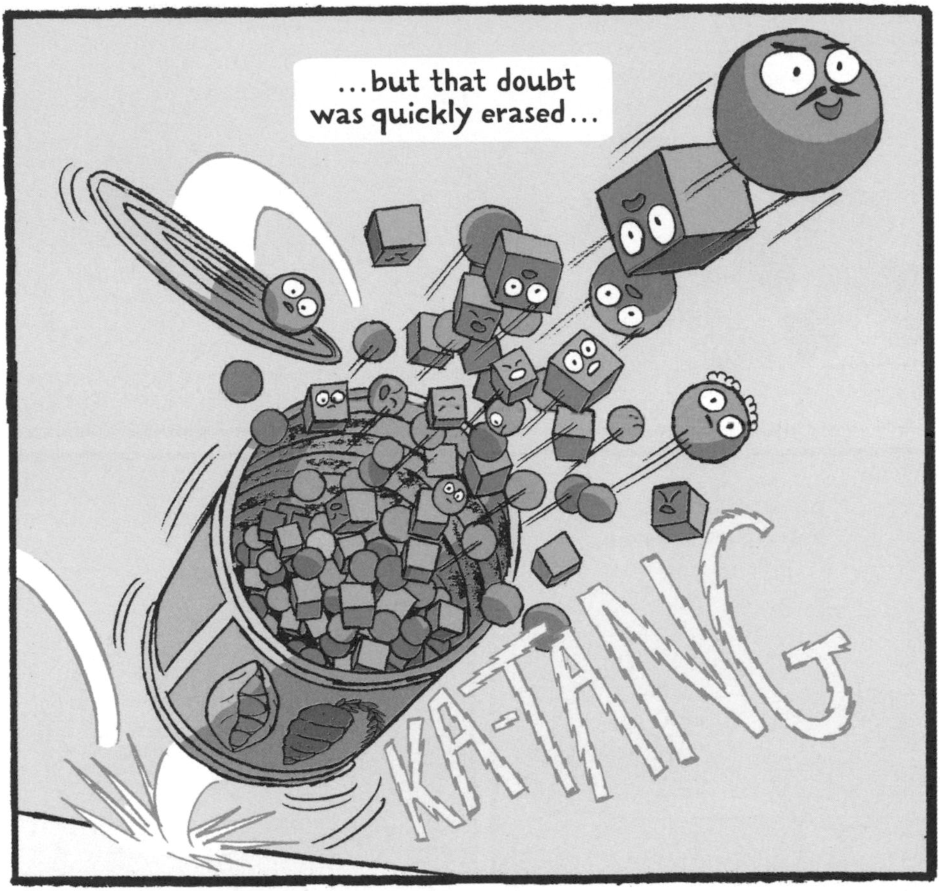
...but that doubt was quickly erased...
KA-TANG

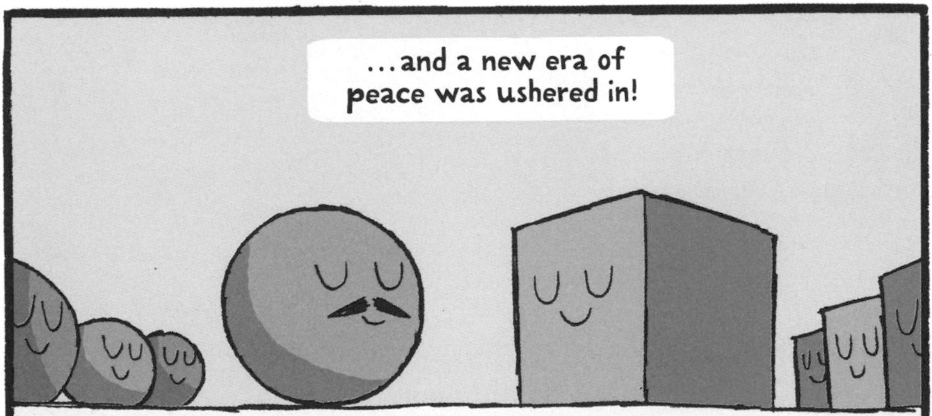
...and a new era of peace was ushered in!

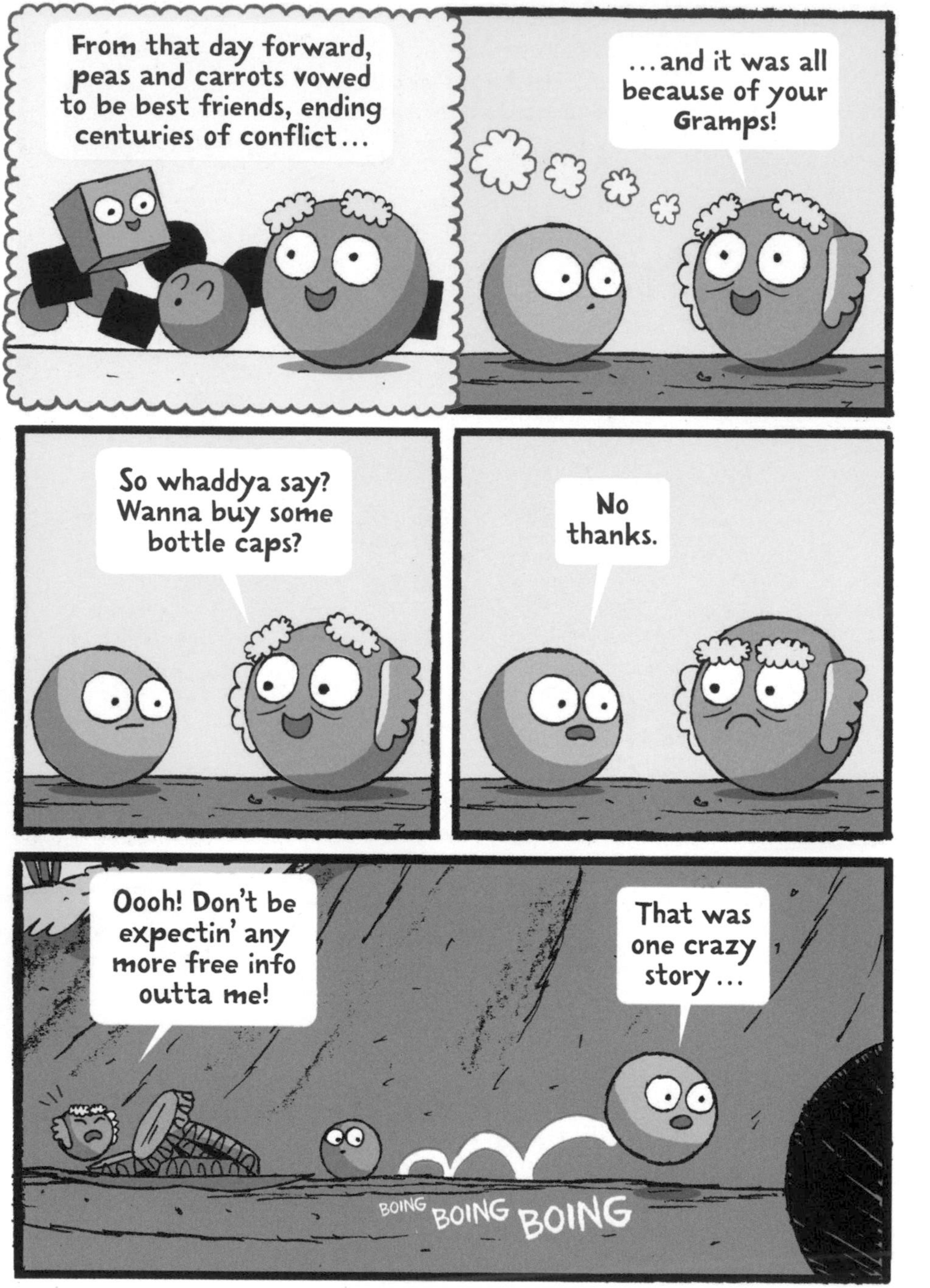
From that day forward, peas and carrots vowed to be best friends, ending centuries of conflict…
…and it was all because of your Gramps!
So whaddya say? Wanna buy some bottle caps?
No thanks.
Oooh! Don't be expectin' any more free info outta me!
That was one crazy story…
BOING BOING BOING

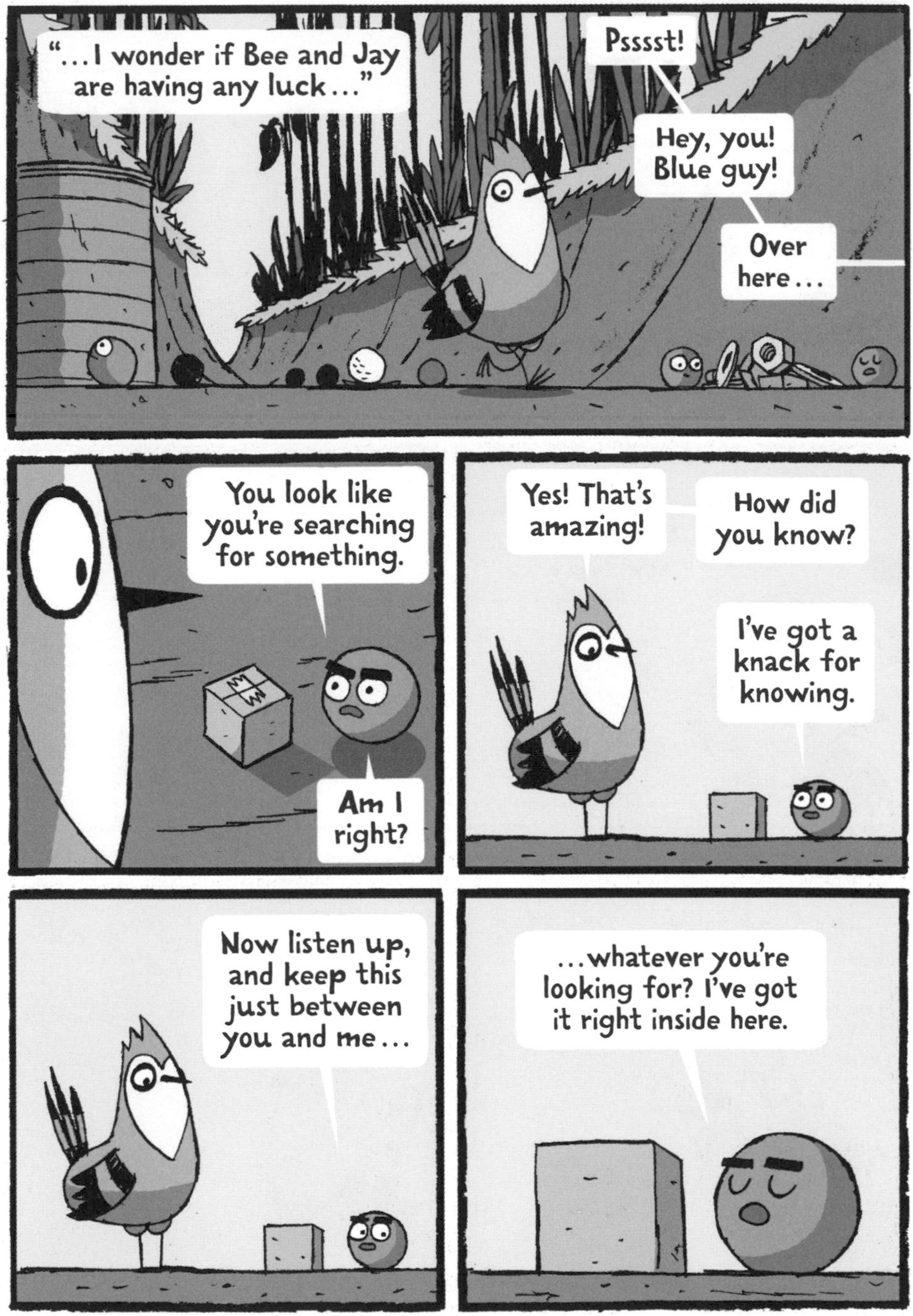
"...I wonder if Bee and Jay are having any luck..."
Psssst!
Hey, you! Blue guy!
Over here...
You look like you're searching for something.
Am I right?
Yes! That's amazing!
How did you know?
I've got a knack for knowing.
Now listen up, and keep this just between you and me...
...whatever you're looking for? I've got it right inside here.

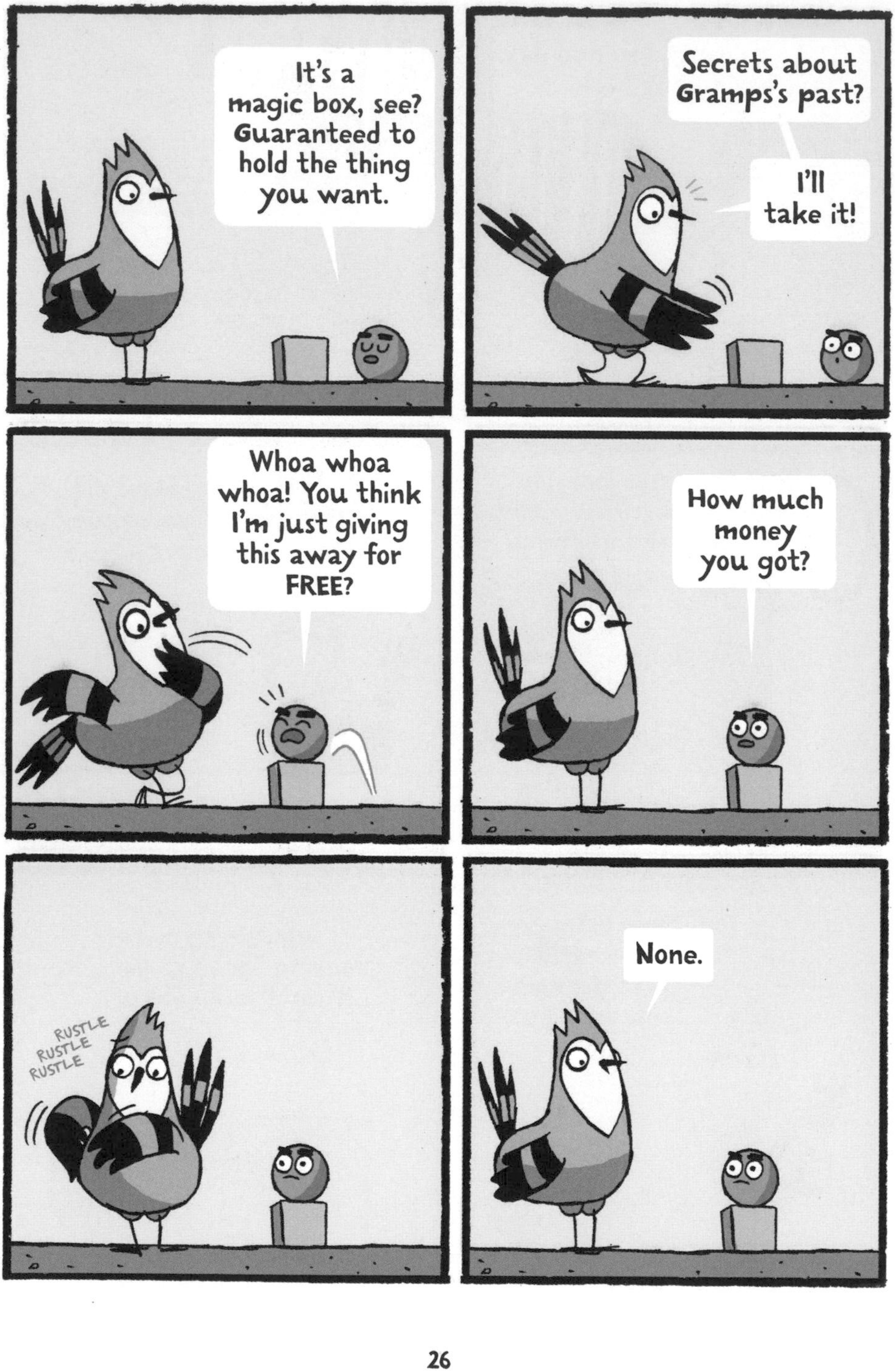

It's a magic box, see? Guaranteed to hold the thing you want.
Secrets about Gramps's past?
I'll take it!
Whoa whoa whoa! You think I'm just giving this away for FREE?
How much money you got?
RUSTLE RUSTLE RUSTLE
None.

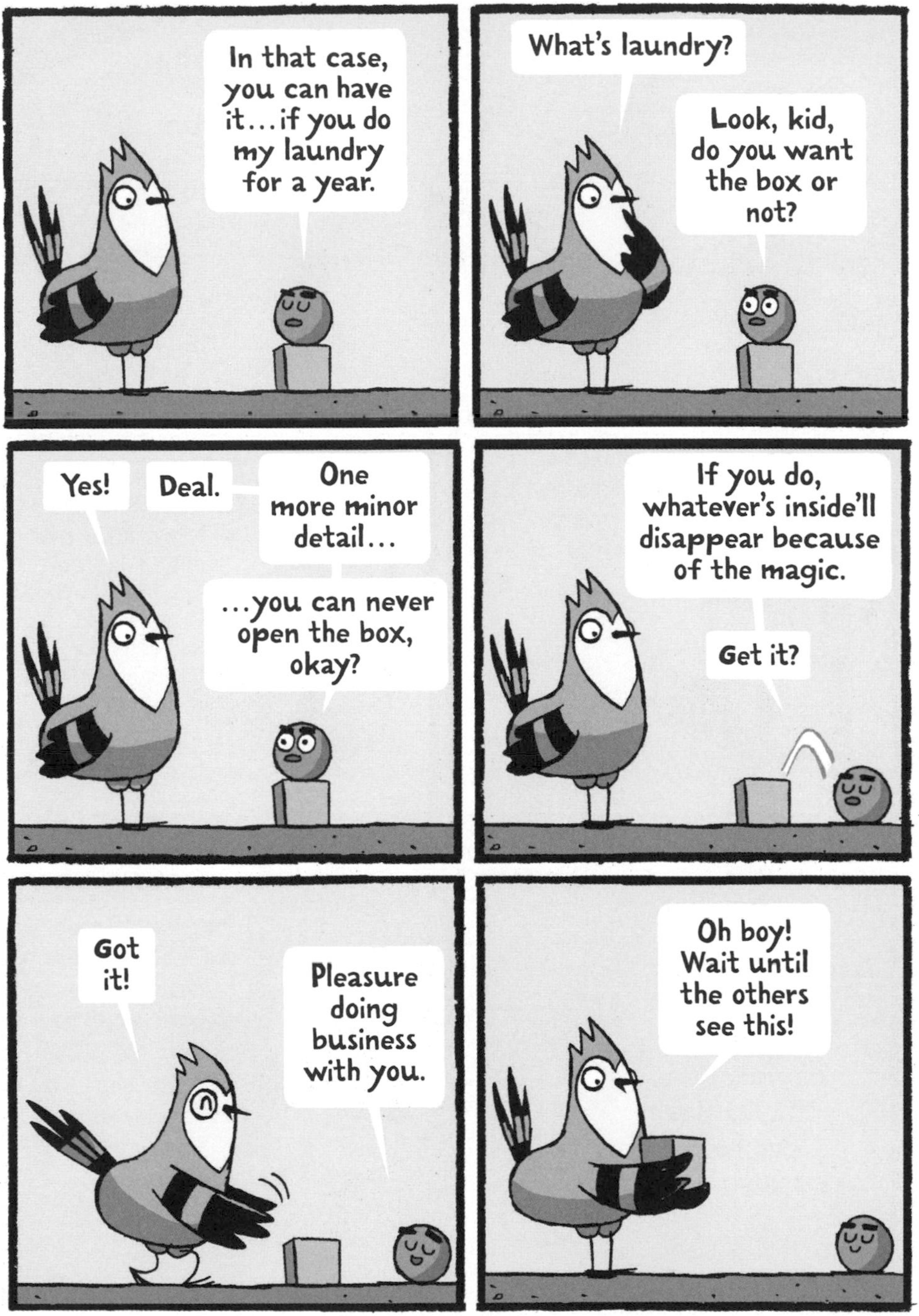
In that case, you can have it...if you do my laundry for a year.
What's laundry?
Look, kid, do you want the box or not?
Yes!
Deal.
One more minor detail...
...you can never open the box, okay?
If you do, whatever's inside'll disappear because of the magic.
Get it?
Got it!
Pleasure doing business with you.
Oh boy! Wait until the others see this!

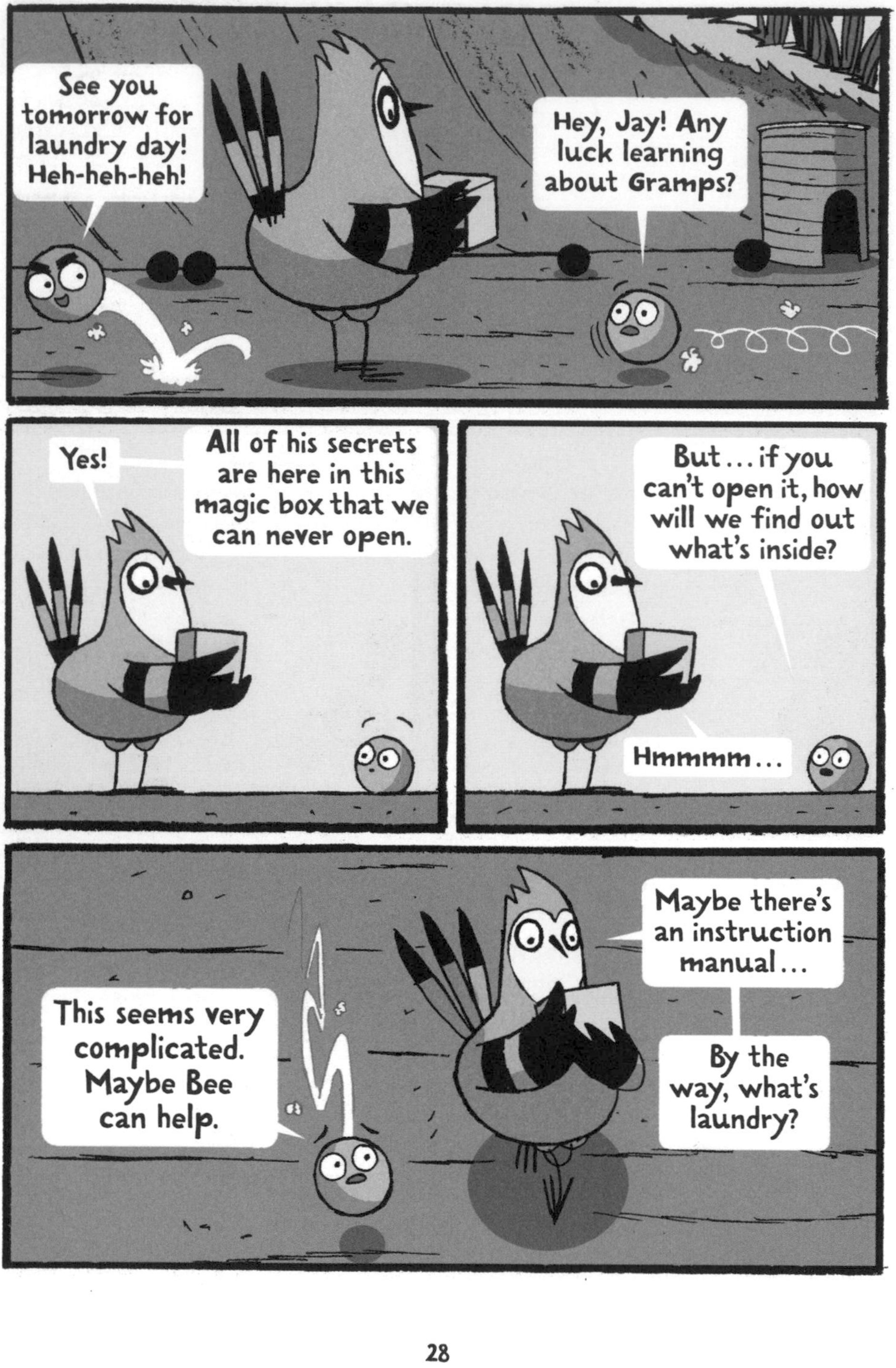
See you tomorrow for laundry day! Heh-heh-heh!
Hey, Jay! Any luck learning about Gramps?
Yes!
All of his secrets are here in this magic box that we can never open.
But... if you can't open it, how will we find out what's inside?
Hmmmm...
Maybe there's an instruction manual...
This seems very complicated. Maybe Bee can help.
By the way, what's laundry?

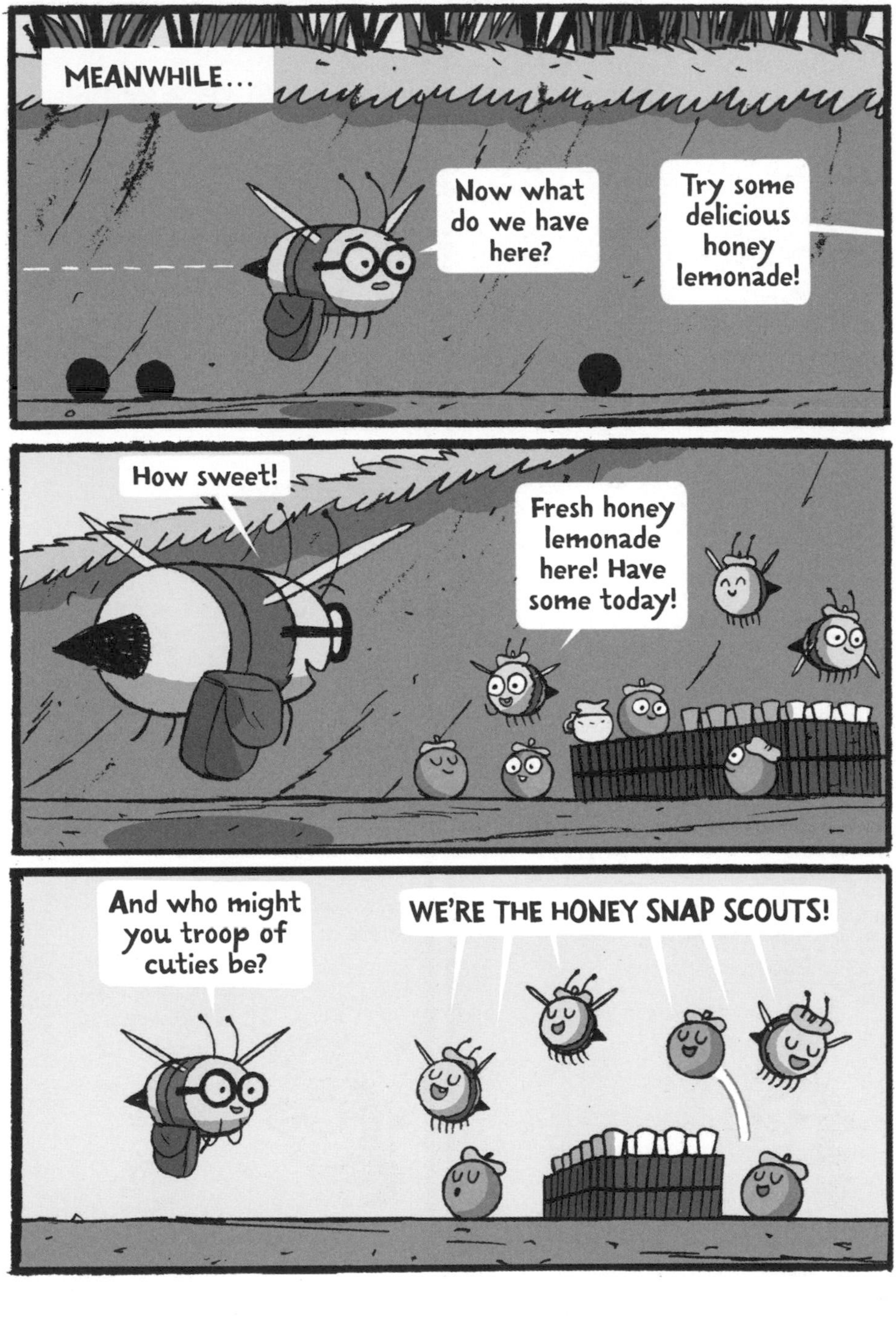
MEANWHILE...
Now what do we have here?
Try some delicious honey lemonade!
How sweet!
Fresh honey lemonade here! Have some today!
And who might you troop of cuties be?
WE'RE THE HONEY SNAP SCOUTS!

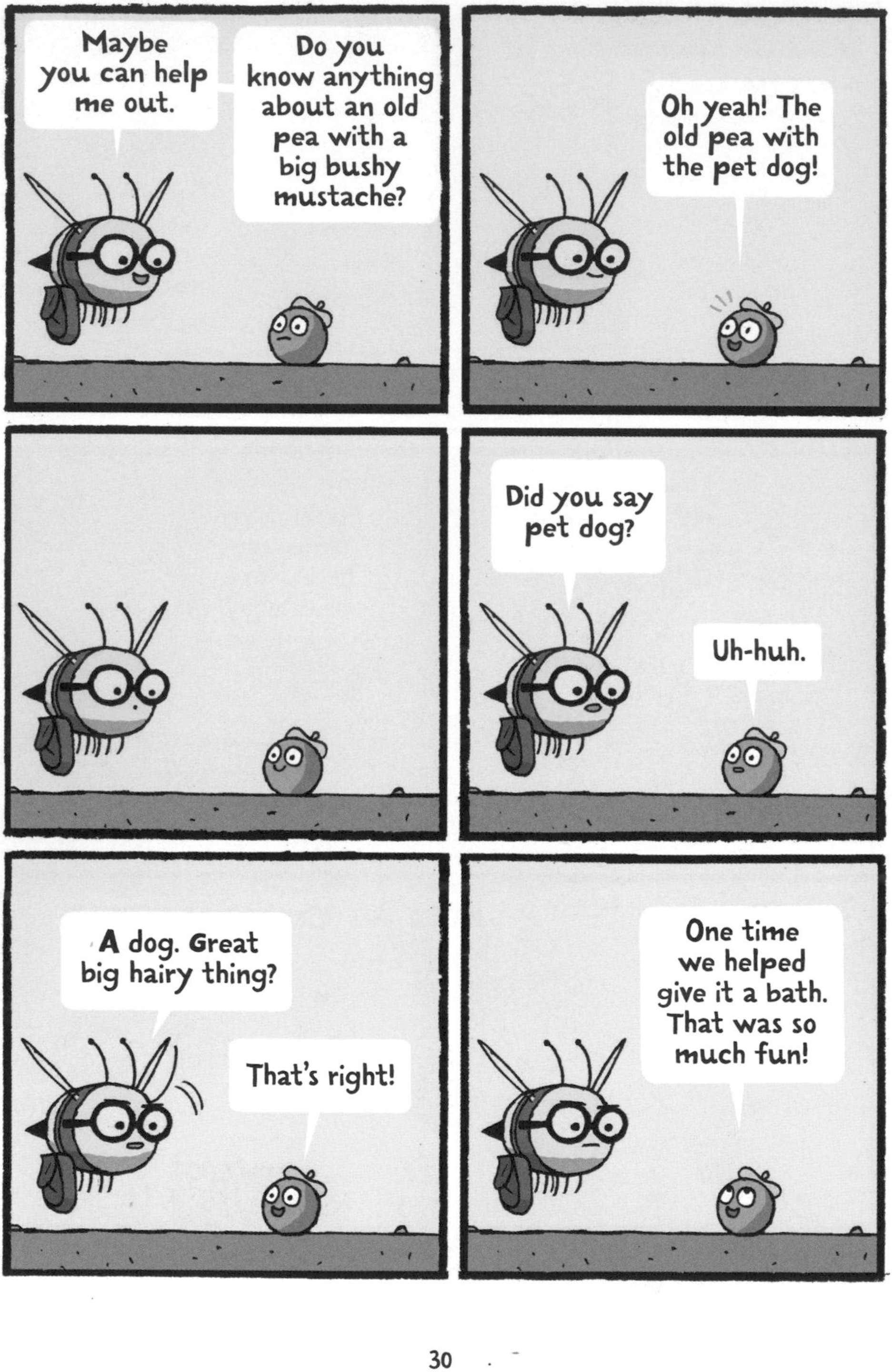
Maybe you can help me out.
Do you know anything about an old pea with a big bushy mustache?
Oh yeah! The old pea with the pet dog!
Did you say pet dog?
Uh-huh.
A dog. Great big hairy thing?
That's right!
One time we helped give it a bath. That was so much fun!

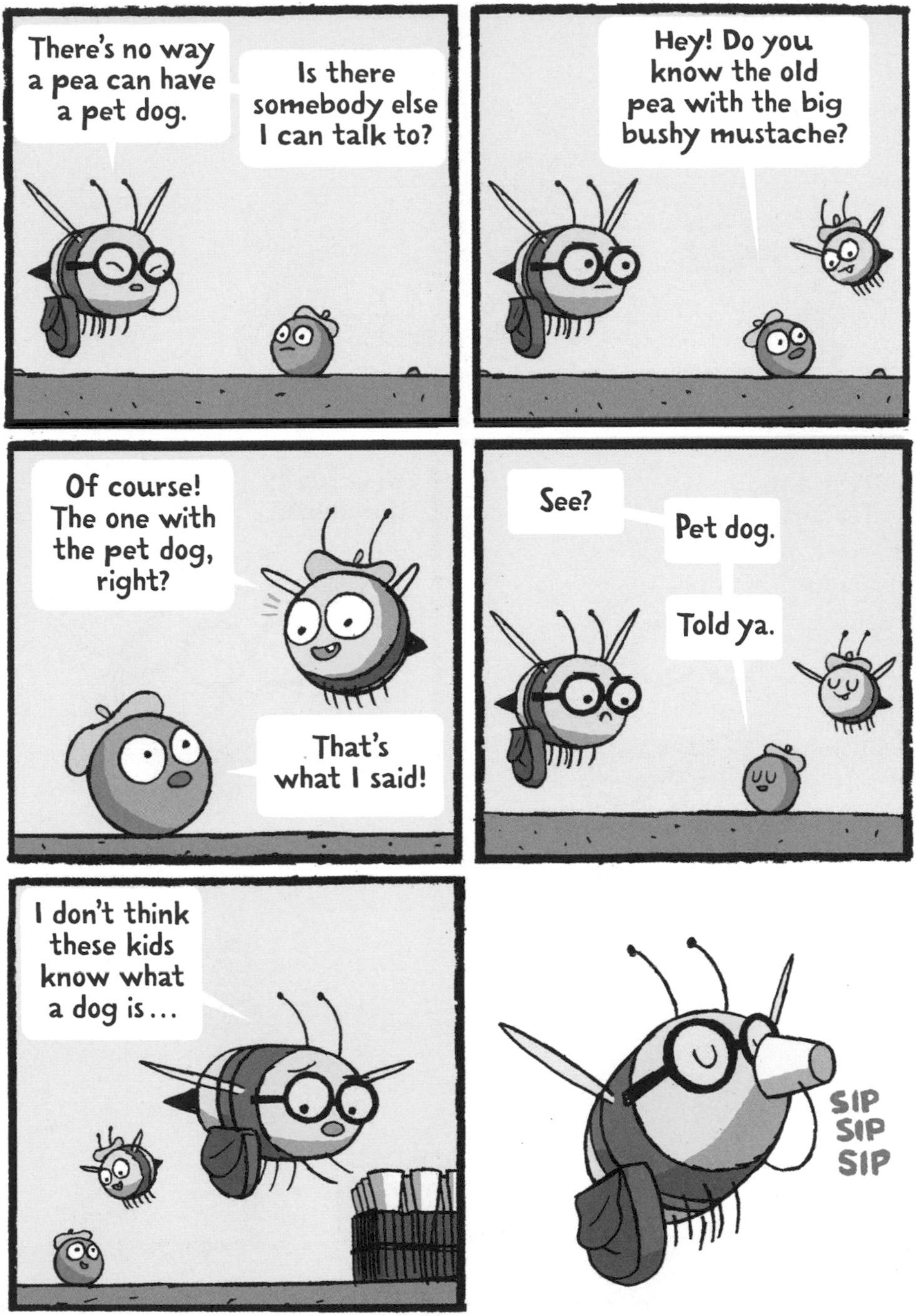
There's no way a pea can have a pet dog.
Is there somebody else I can talk to?
Hey! Do you know the old pea with the big bushy mustache?
Of course! The one with the pet dog, right?
That's what I said!
See?
Pet dog.
Told ya.
I don't think these kids know what a dog is...
SIP SIP SIP

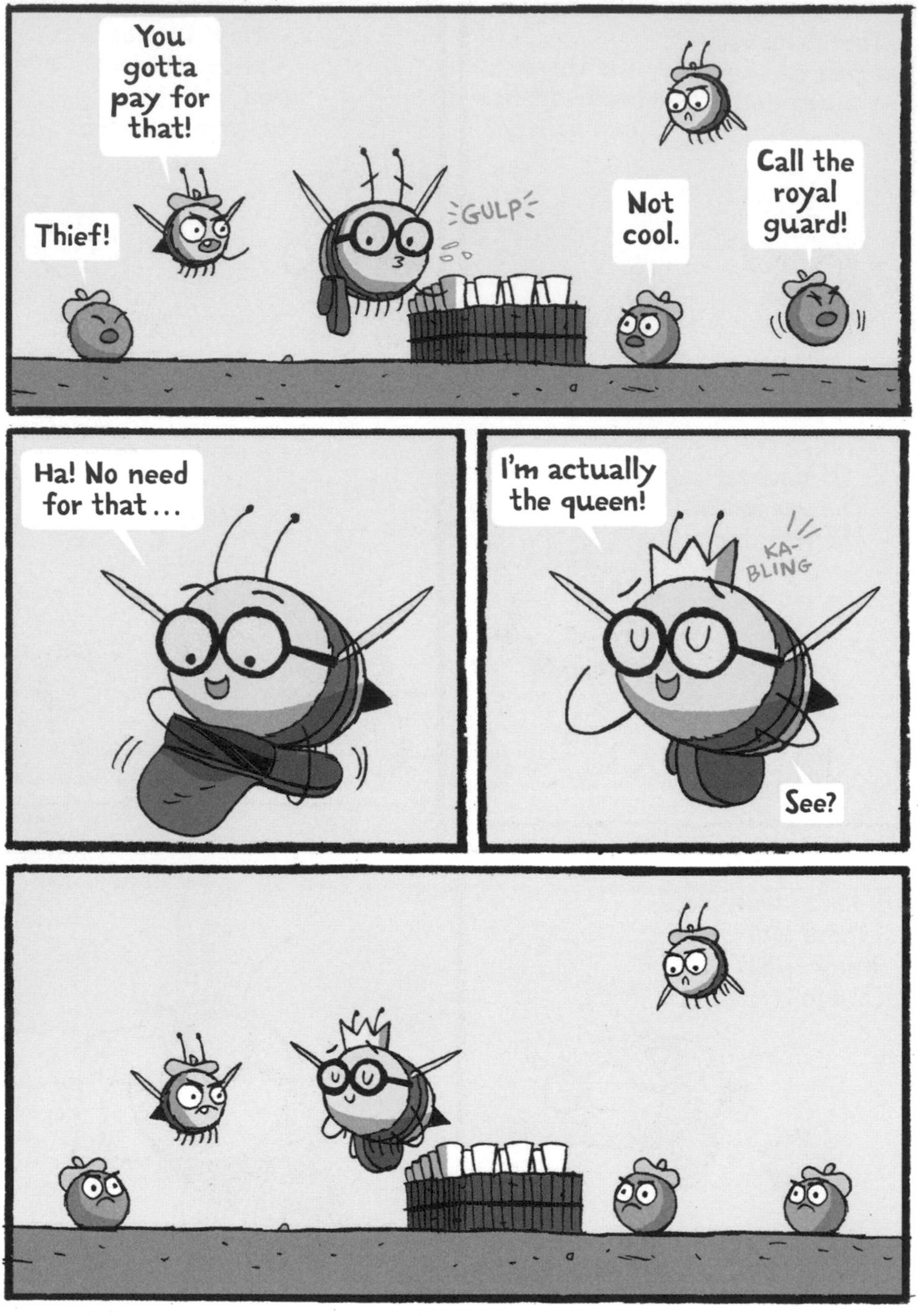
Thief!
You gotta pay for that!
GULP
Not cool.
Call the royal guard!
Ha! No need for that...
I'm actually the queen!
KA-BLING
See?

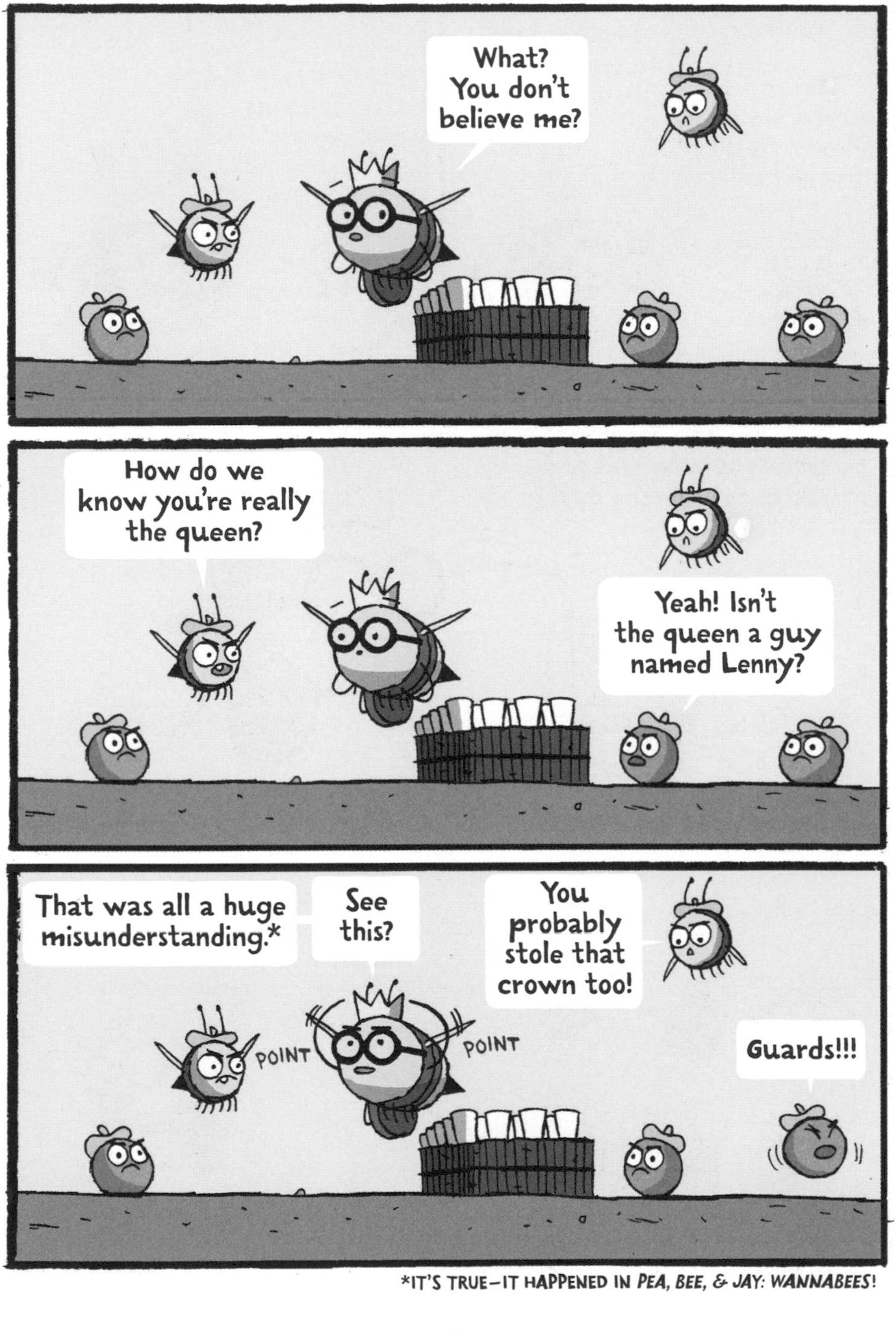
What? You don't believe me?
How do we know you're really the queen?
Yeah! Isn't the queen a guy named Lenny?
That was all a huge misunderstanding.*
See this?
You probably stole that crown too!
POINT
POINT
Guards!!!

*IT'S TRUE—IT HAPPENED IN *PEA, BEE, & JAY: WANNABEES!*

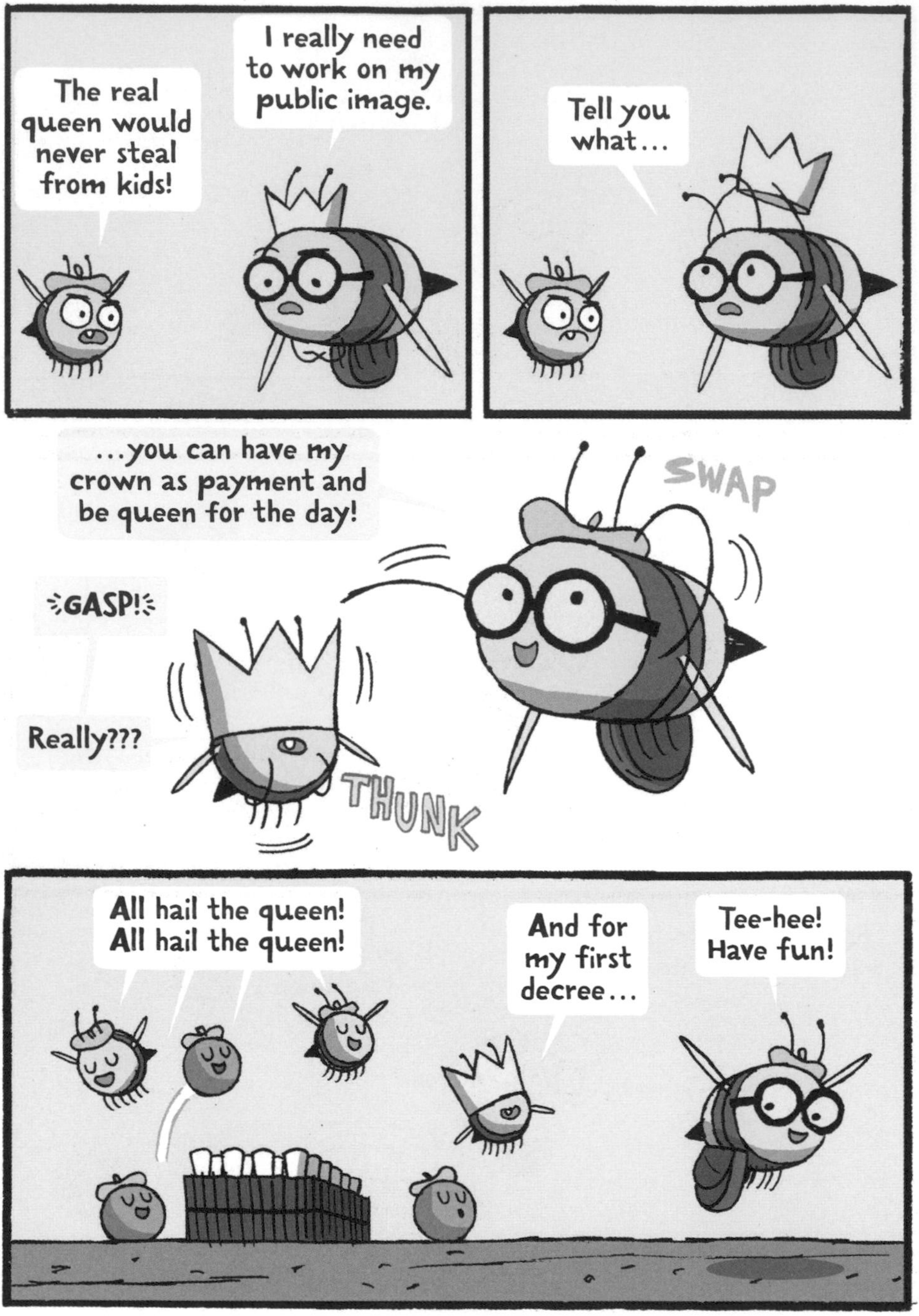
The real queen would never steal from kids!
I really need to work on my public image.
Tell you what...
...you can have my crown as payment and be queen for the day!
SWAP
GASP!
Really???
THUNK
All hail the queen! All hail the queen!
And for my first decree...
Tee-hee! Have fun!

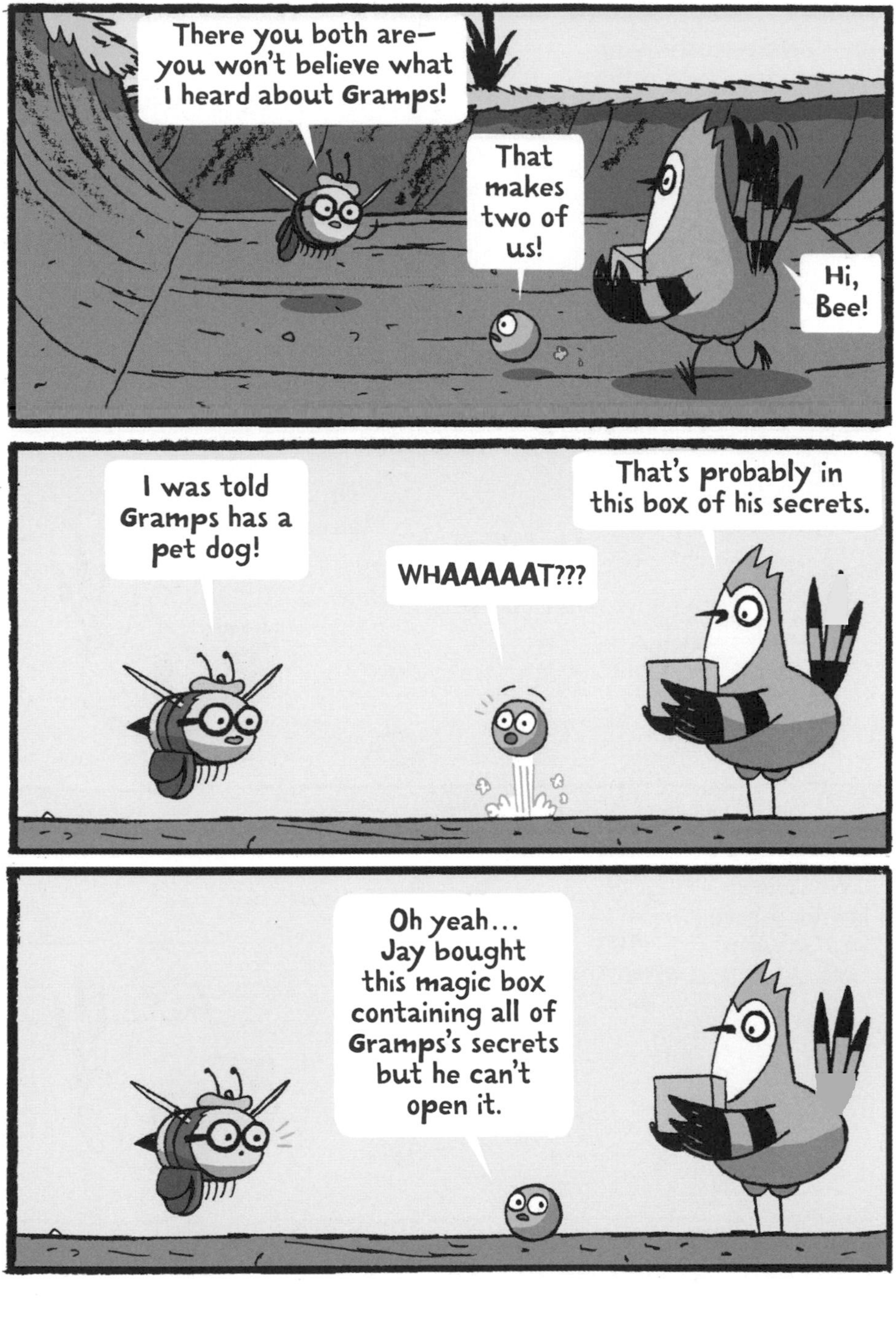
There you both are—you won't believe what I heard about Gramps!
That makes two of us!
Hi, Bee!
I was told Gramps has a pet dog!
WHAAAAAT???
That's probably in this box of his secrets.
Oh yeah… Jay bought this magic box containing all of Gramps's secrets but he can't open it.

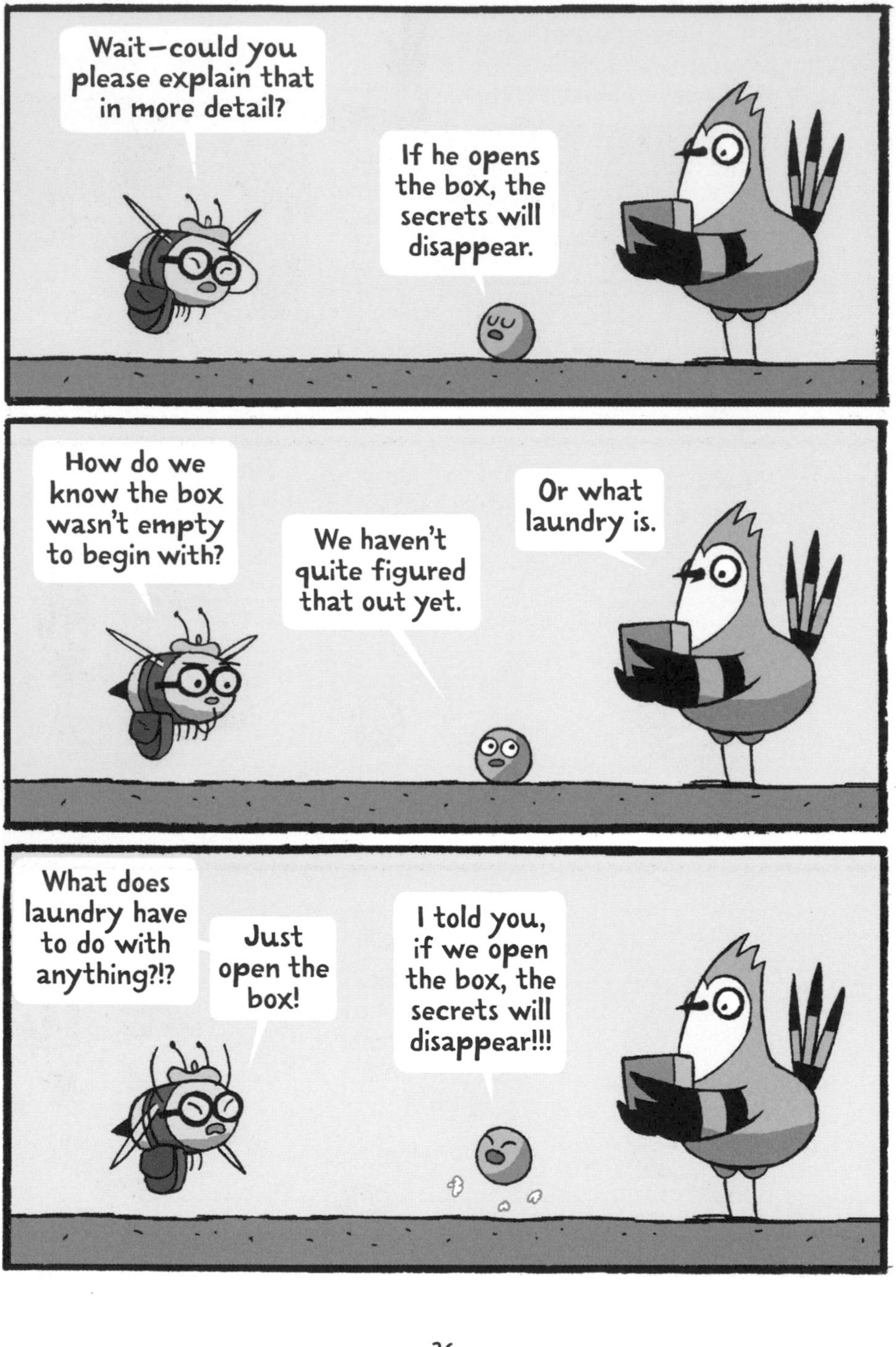
Wait—could you please explain that in more detail?
If he opens the box, the secrets will disappear.
How do we know the box wasn't empty to begin with?
We haven't quite figured that out yet.
Or what laundry is.
What does laundry have to do with anything?!?
Just open the box!
I told you, if we open the box, the secrets will disappear!!!

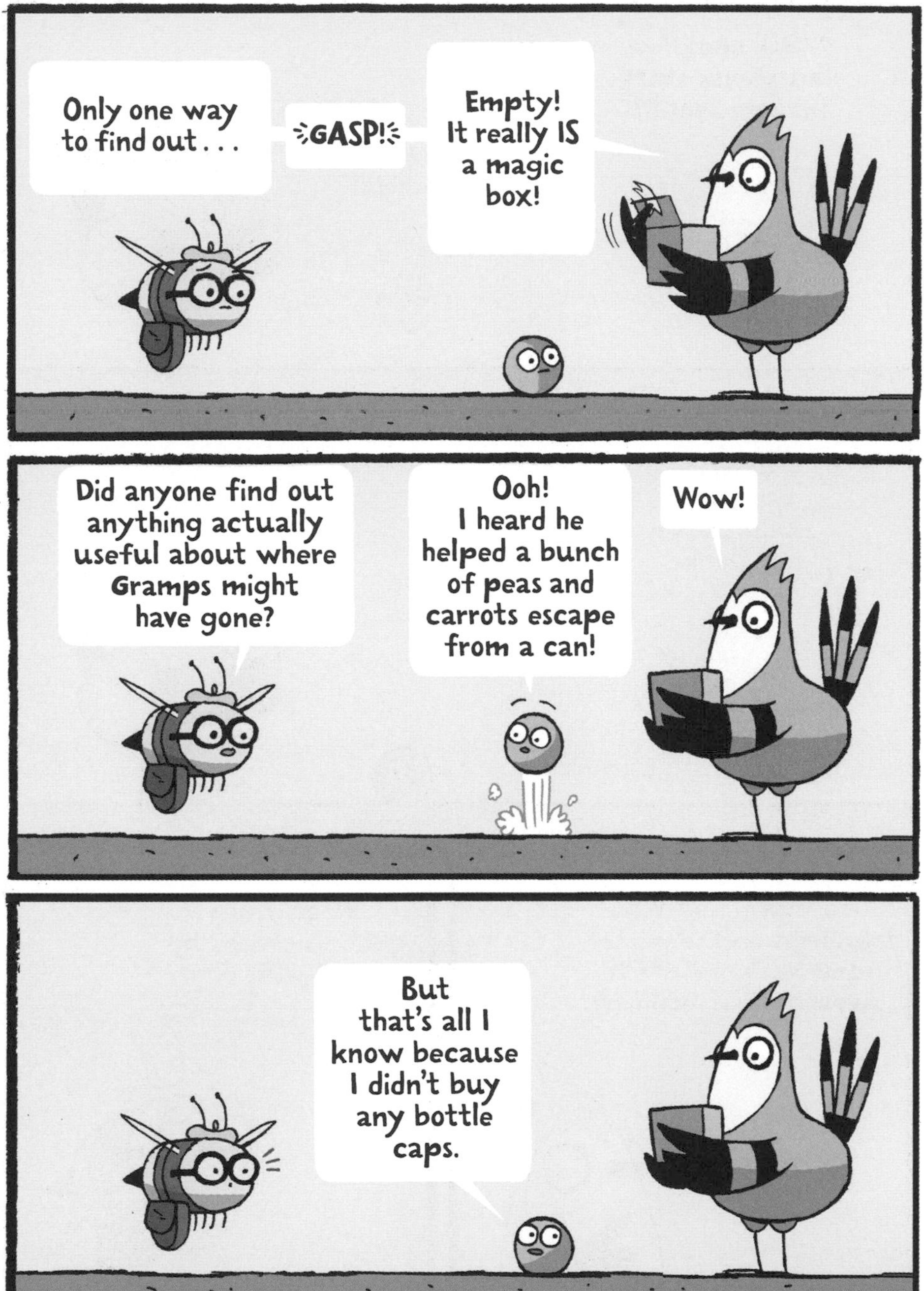
Only one way to find out . . .
GASP!
Empty! It really IS a magic box!
Did anyone find out anything actually useful about where Gramps might have gone?
Ooh! I heard he helped a bunch of peas and carrots escape from a can!
Wow!
But that's all I know because I didn't buy any bottle caps.

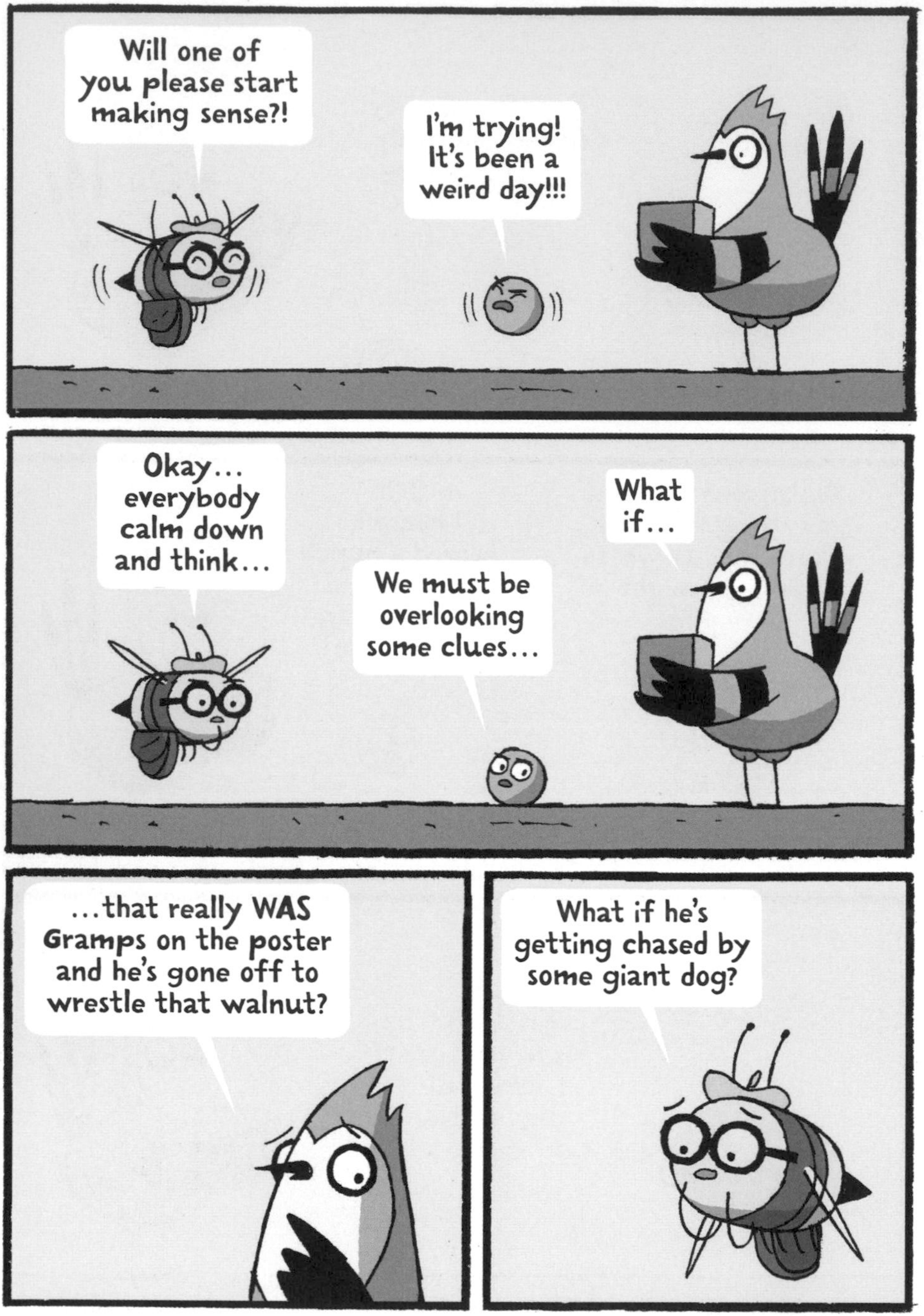

Will one of you please start making sense?!
I'm trying! It's been a weird day!!!
Okay... everybody calm down and think...
We must be overlooking some clues...
What if...
...that really WAS Gramps on the poster and he's gone off to wrestle that walnut?
What if he's getting chased by some giant dog?

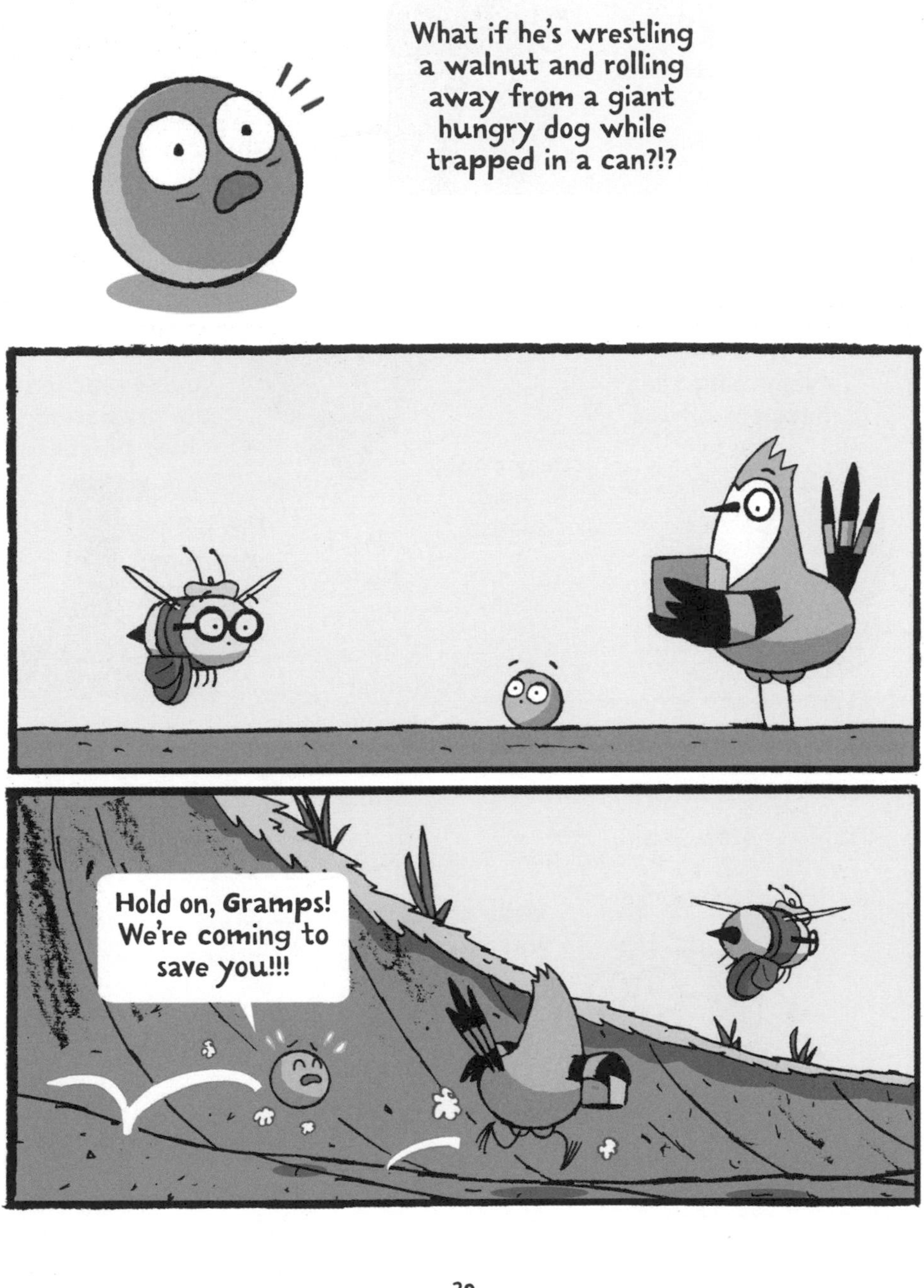
What if he's wrestling a walnut and rolling away from a giant hungry dog while trapped in a can?!?
Hold on, Gramps! We're coming to save you!!!

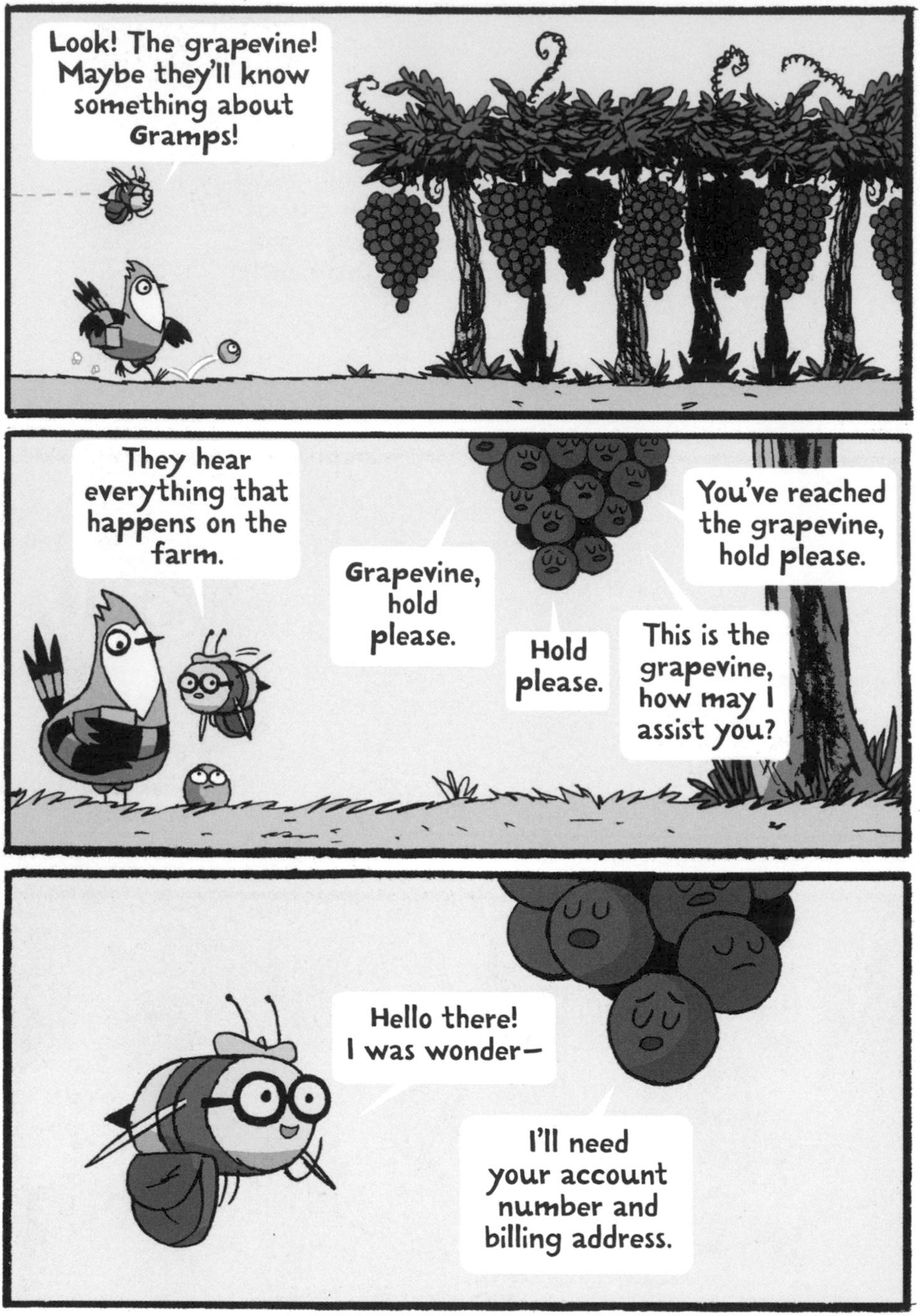

Look! The grapevine! Maybe they'll know something about Gramps!
They hear everything that happens on the farm.
Grapevine, hold please.
Hold please.
You've reached the grapevine, hold please.
This is the grapevine, how may I assist you?
Hello there! I was wonder—
I'll need your account number and billing address.

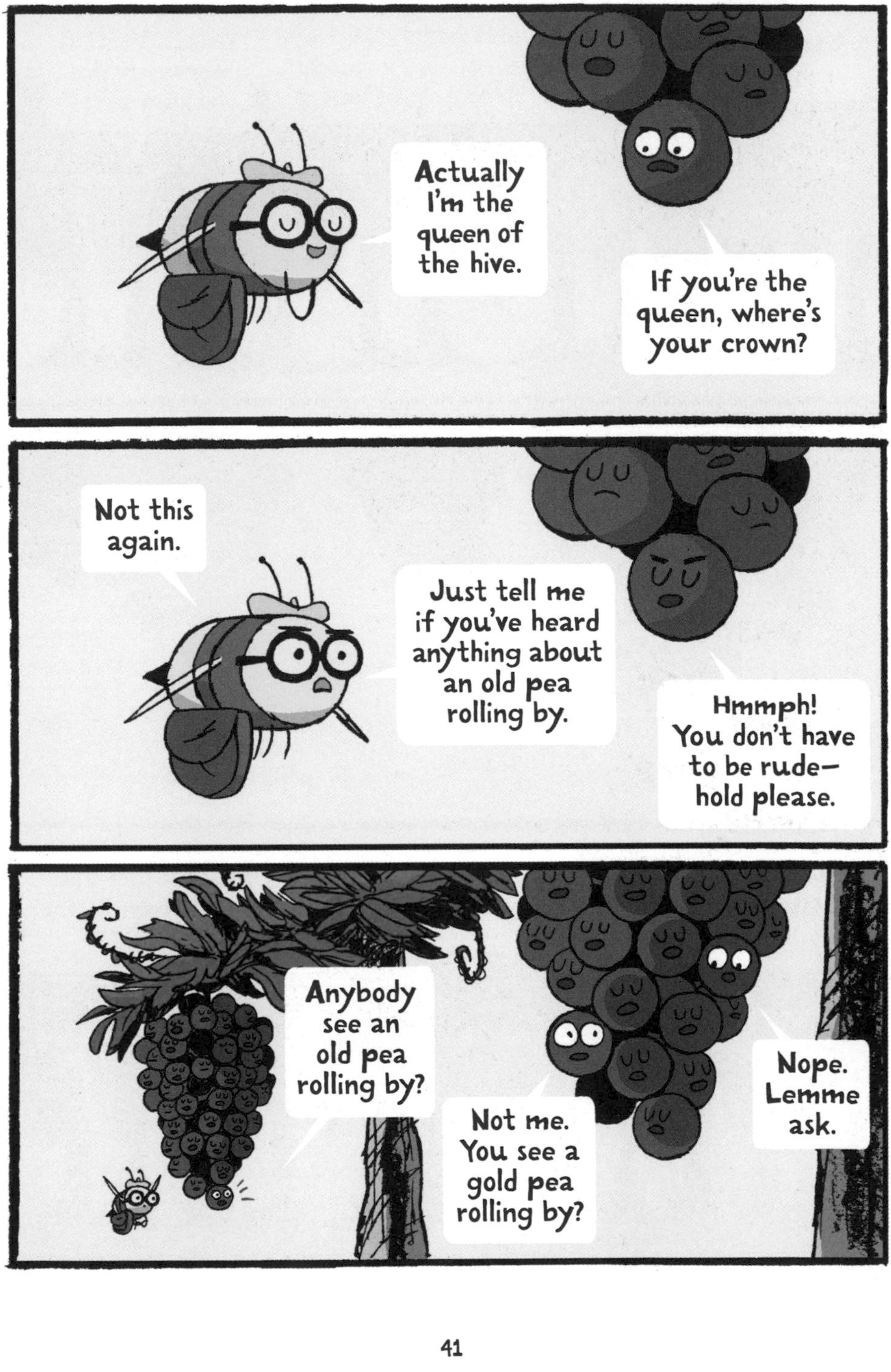
Actually I'm the queen of the hive.
If you're the queen, where's your crown?
Not this again.
Just tell me if you've heard anything about an old pea rolling by.
Hmmph! You don't have to be rude— hold please.
Anybody see an old pea rolling by?
Not me. You see a gold pea rolling by?
Nope. Lemme ask.

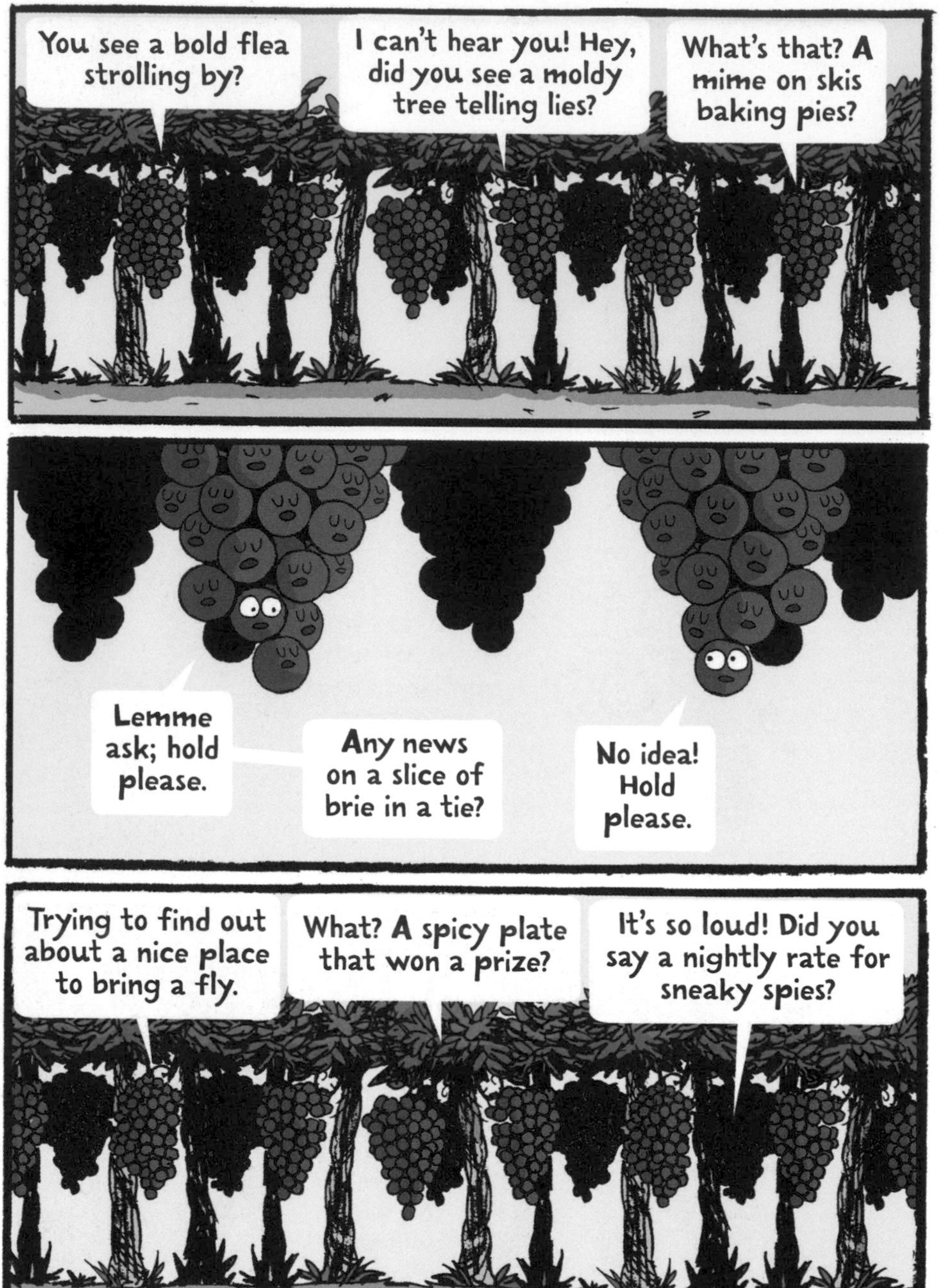

You see a bold flea strolling by?
I can't hear you! Hey, did you see a moldy tree telling lies?
What's that? A mime on skis baking pies?
Lemme ask; hold please.
Any news on a slice of brie in a tie?
No idea! Hold please.
Trying to find out about a nice place to bring a fly.
What? A spicy plate that won a prize?
It's so loud! Did you say a nightly rate for sneaky spies?

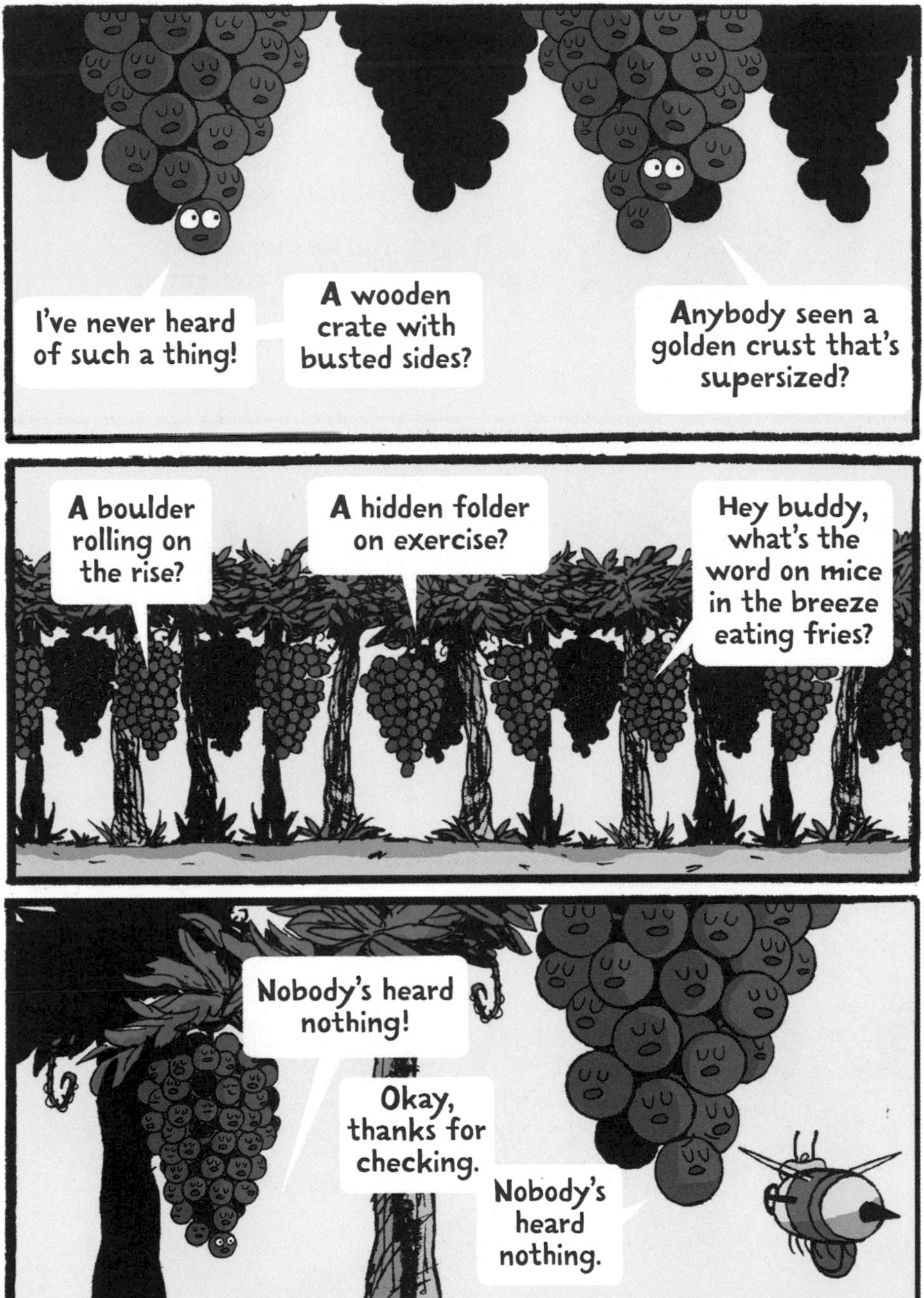
I've never heard of such a thing!
A wooden crate with busted sides?
Anybody seen a golden crust that's supersized?
A boulder rolling on the rise?
A hidden folder on exercise?
Hey buddy, what's the word on mice in the breeze eating fries?
Nobody's heard nothing!
Okay, thanks for checking.
Nobody's heard nothing.

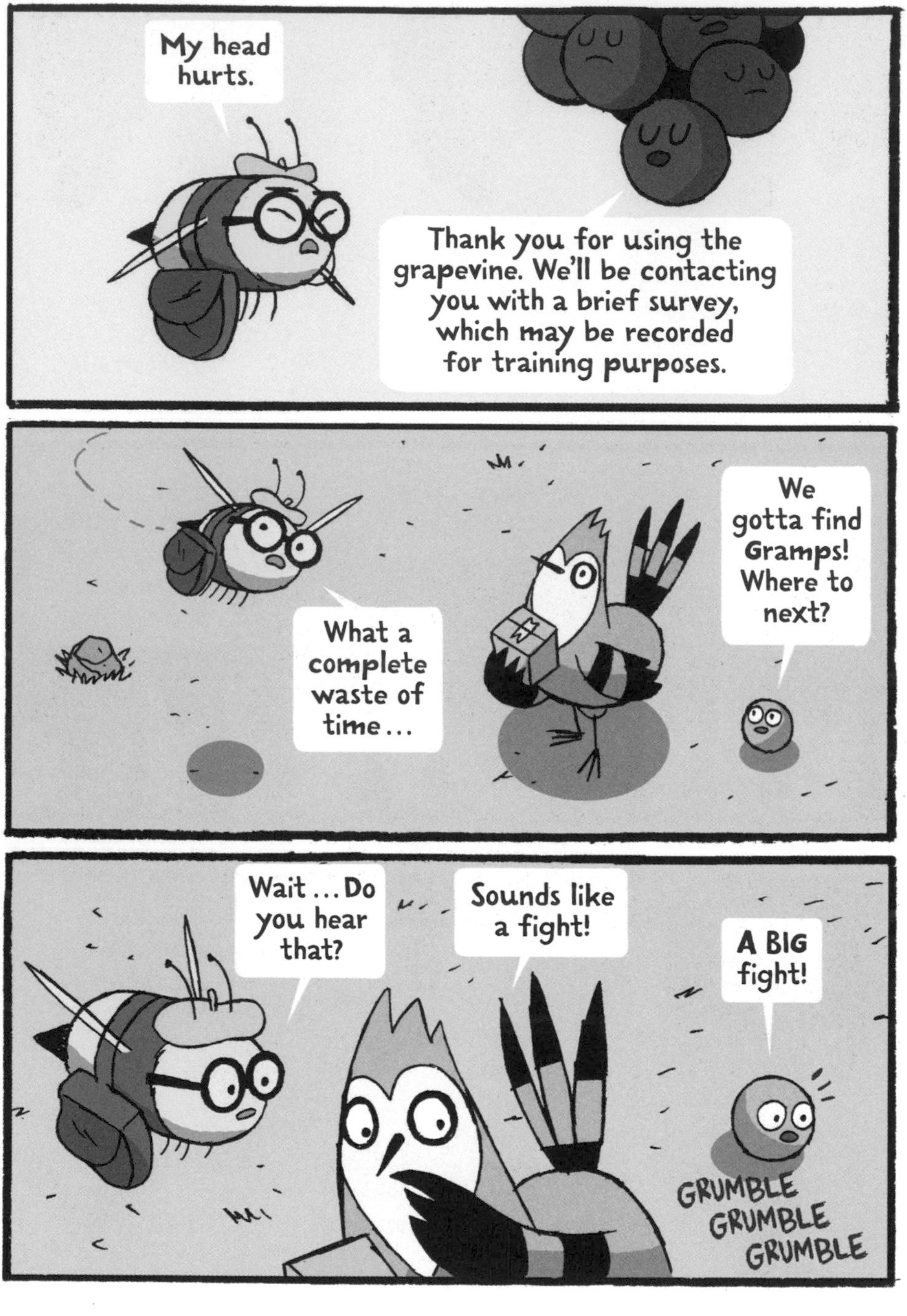
My head hurts.
Thank you for using the grapevine. We'll be contacting you with a brief survey, which may be recorded for training purposes.
What a complete waste of time...
We gotta find Gramps! Where to next?
Wait... Do you hear that?
Sounds like a fight!
A BIG fight!
GRUMBLE GRUMBLE GRUMBLE

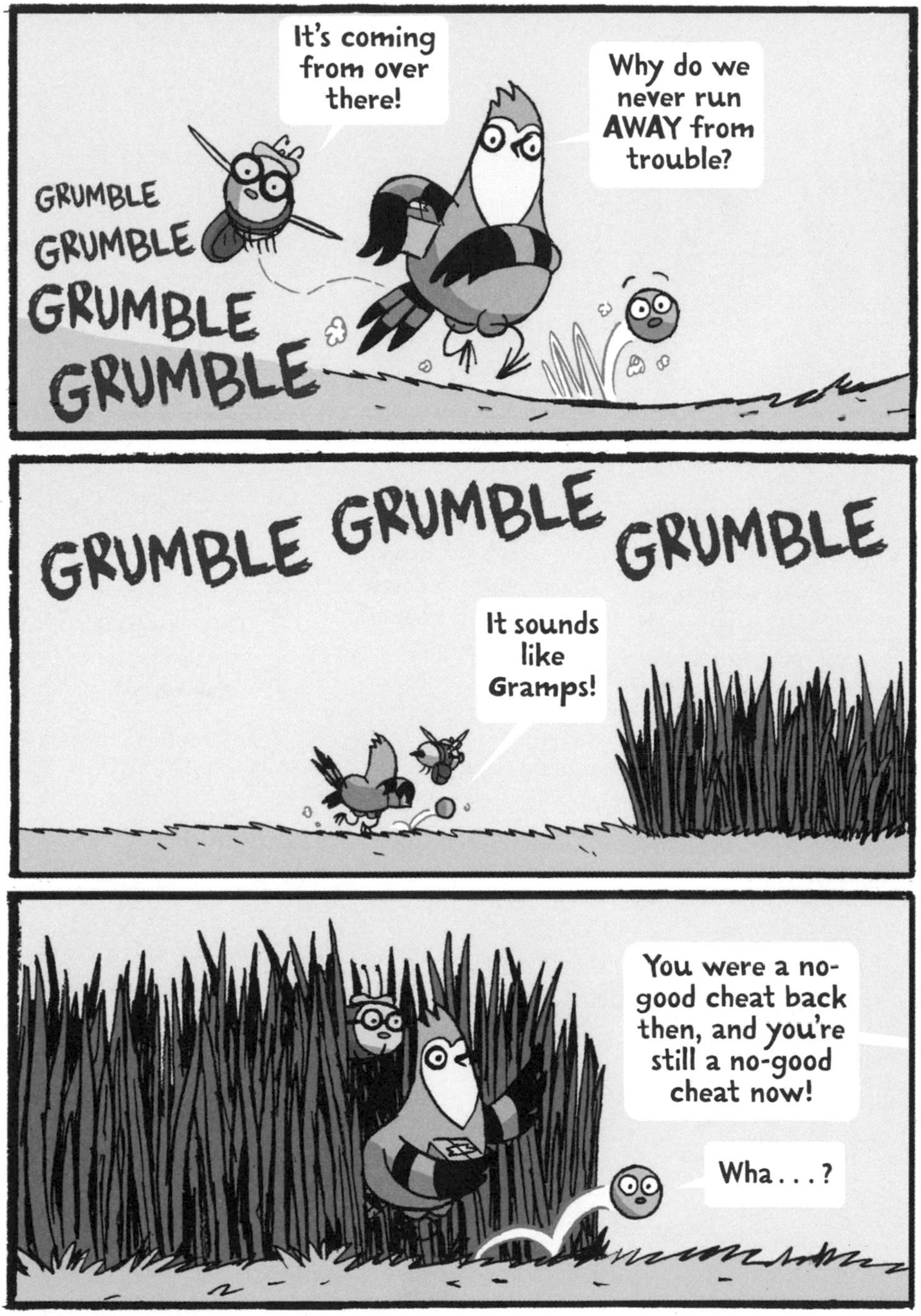

GRUMBLE
GRUMBLE
GRUMBLE
GRUMBLE
It's coming from over there!
Why do we never run AWAY from trouble?
GRUMBLE GRUMBLE GRUMBLE
It sounds like Gramps!
You were a no-good cheat back then, and you're still a no-good cheat now!
Wha . . . ?

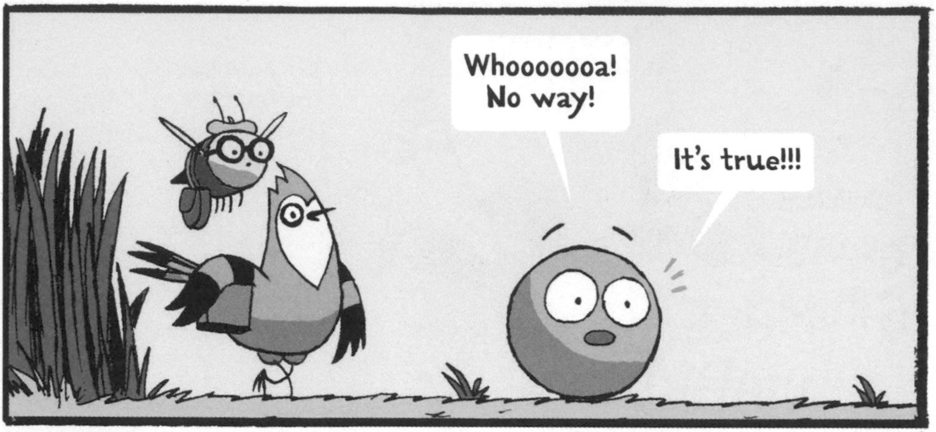
Whoooooa! No way!
It's true!!!
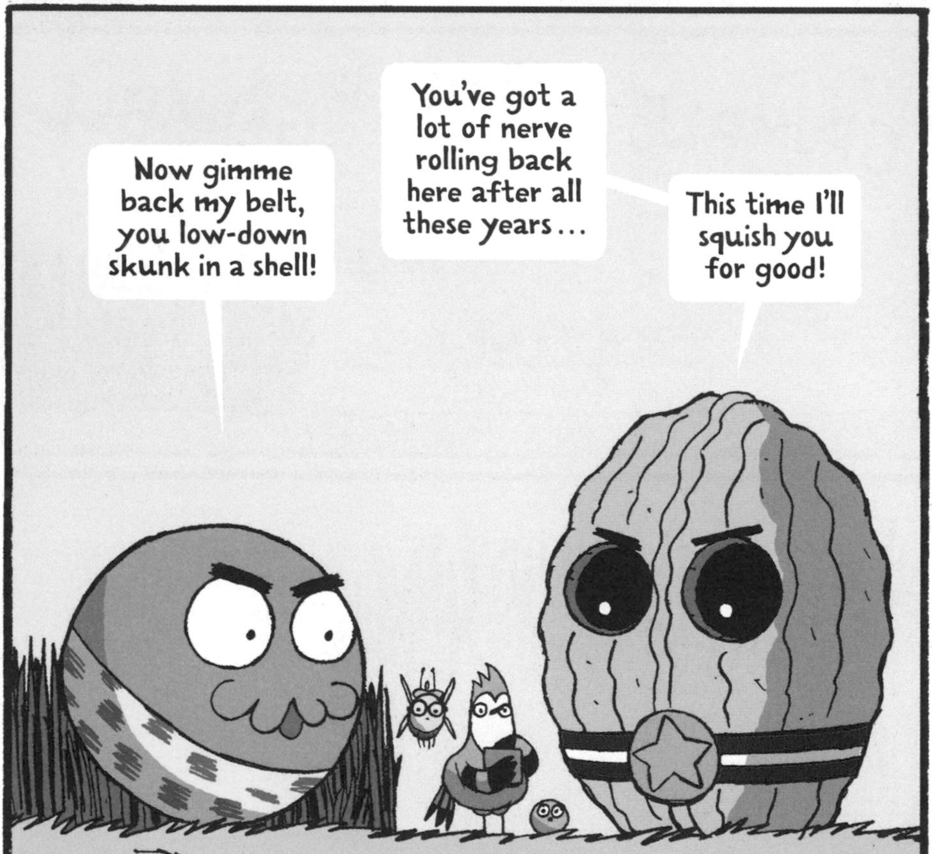
Now gimme back my belt, you low-down skunk in a shell!
You've got a lot of nerve rolling back here after all these years...
This time I'll squish you for good!

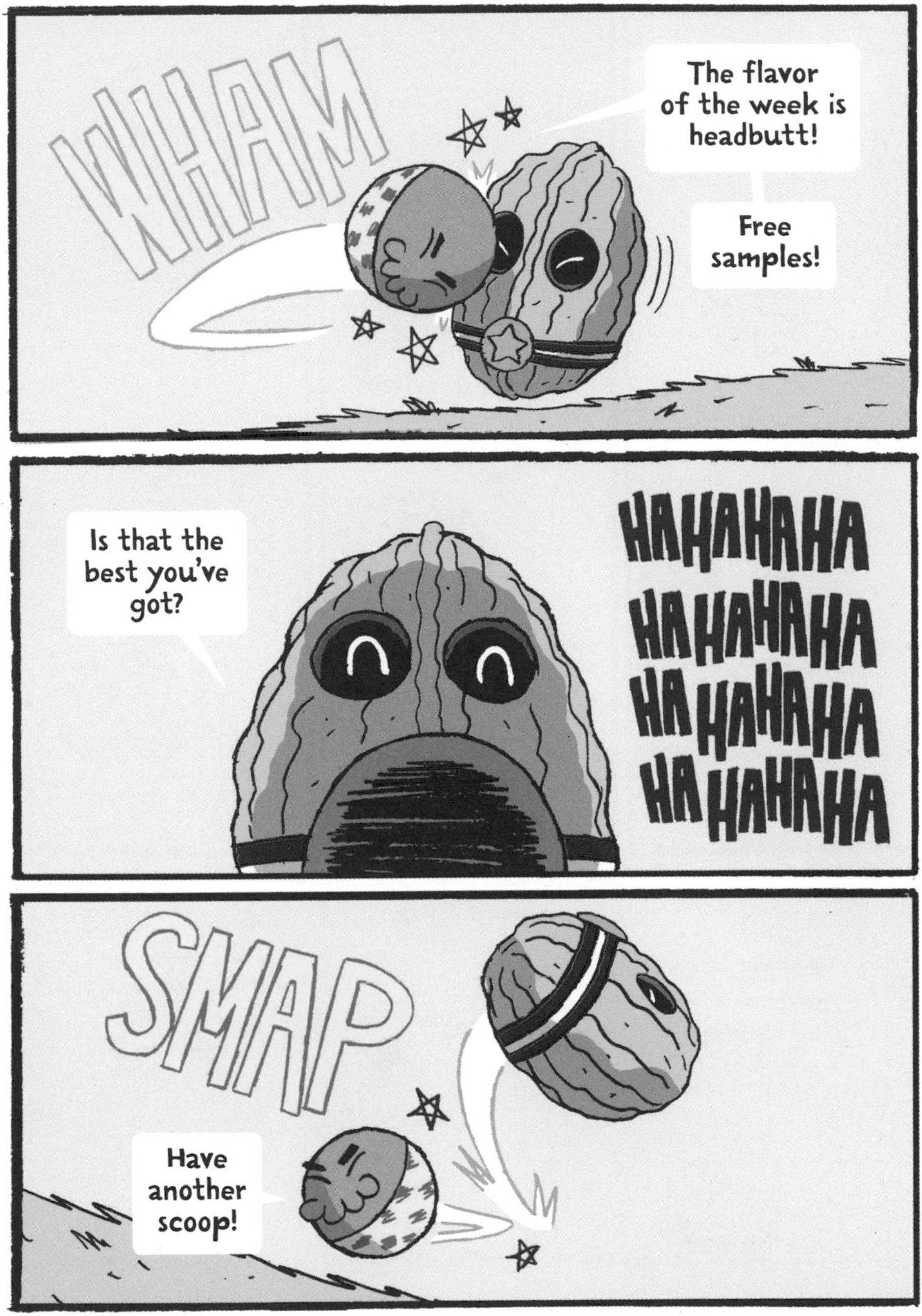
WHAM
The flavor of the week is headbutt!
Free samples!
Is that the best you've got?
HAHAHAHA
HAHAHAHA
HAHAHAHA
HAHAHAHA
SMAP
Have another scoop!

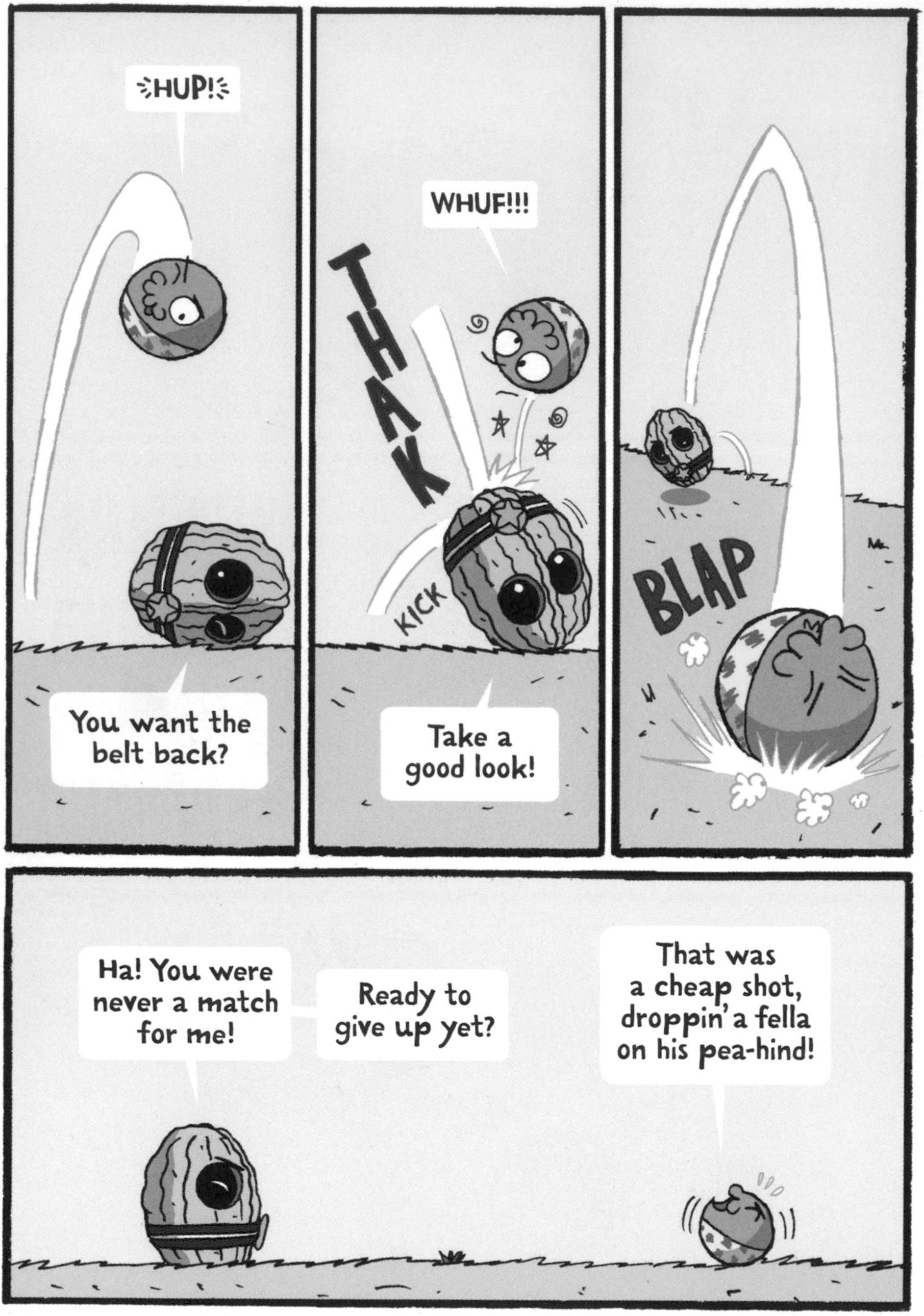
HUP!
You want the belt back?
WHUF!!!
THAK
KICK
Take a good look!
BLAP
Ha! You were never a match for me!
Ready to give up yet?
That was a cheap shot, droppin' a fella on his pea-hind!

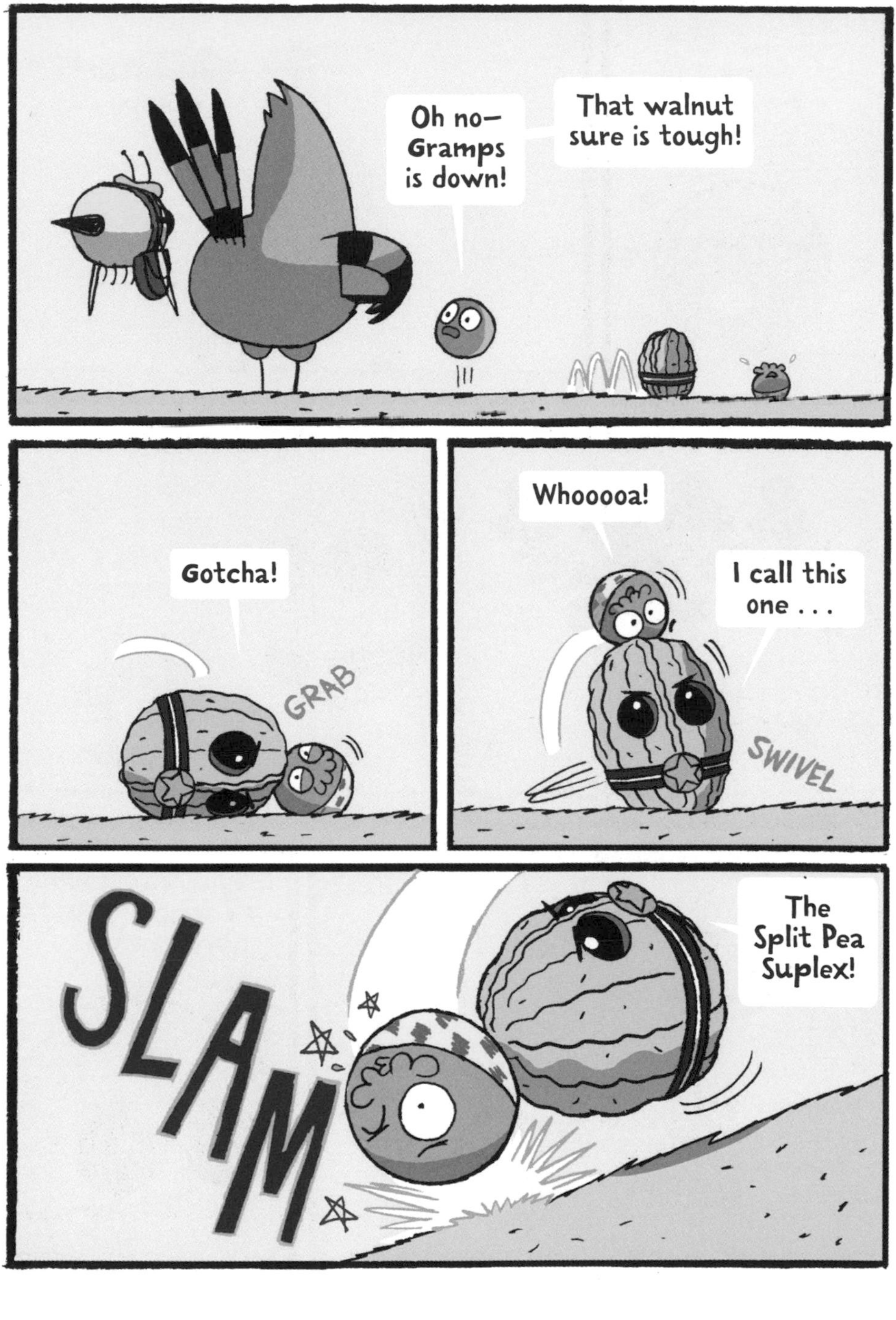
Oh no—
Gramps
is down!
That walnut
sure is tough!
Gotcha!
GRAB
Whooooa!
I call this
one . . .
SWIVEL
SLAM
The
Split Pea
Suplex!

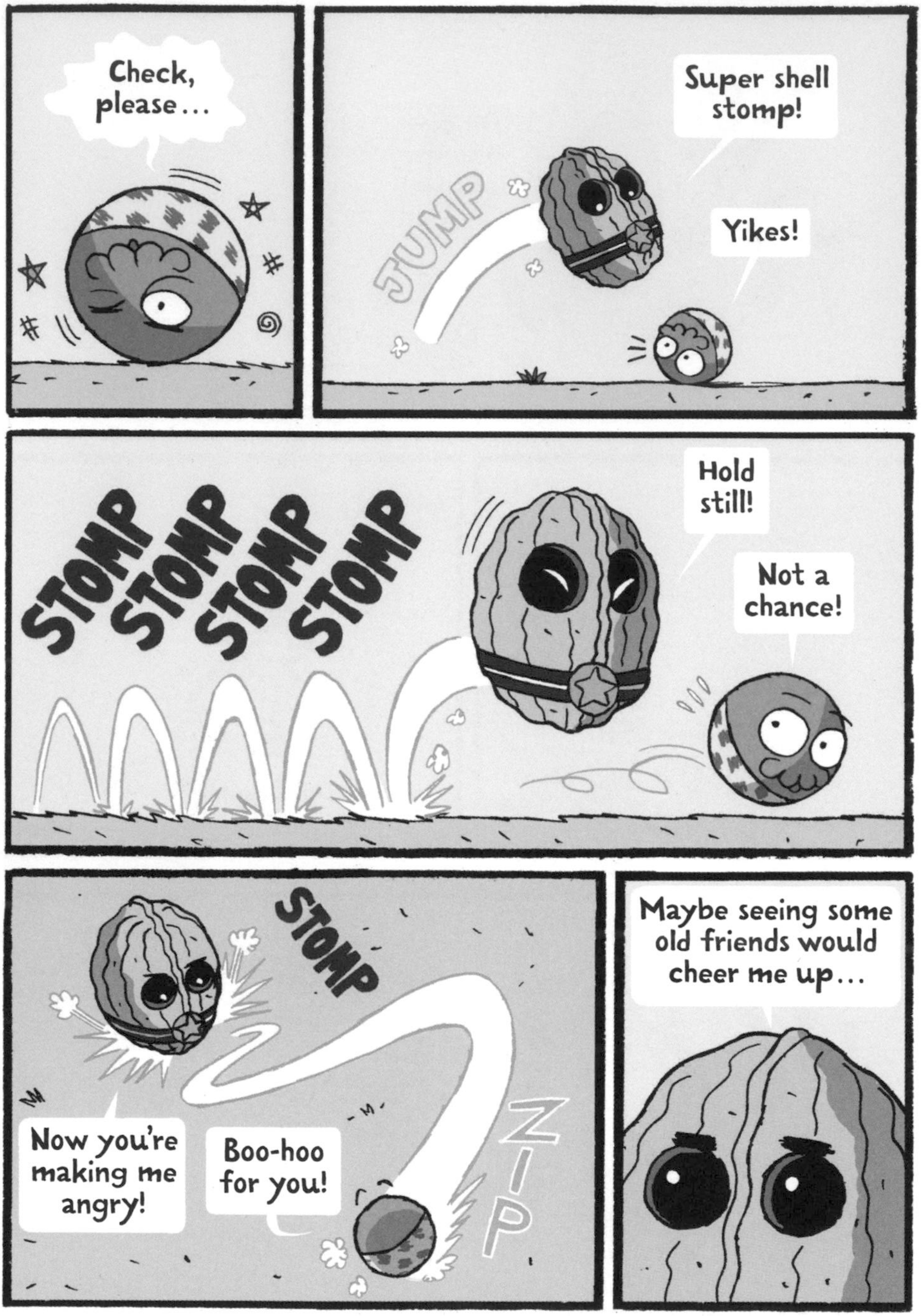
Check, please...
Super shell stomp!
JUMP
Yikes!
STOMP STOMP STOMP STOMP
Hold still!
Not a chance!
STOMP
Now you're making me angry!
Boo-hoo for you!
ZIP
Maybe seeing some old friends would cheer me up...

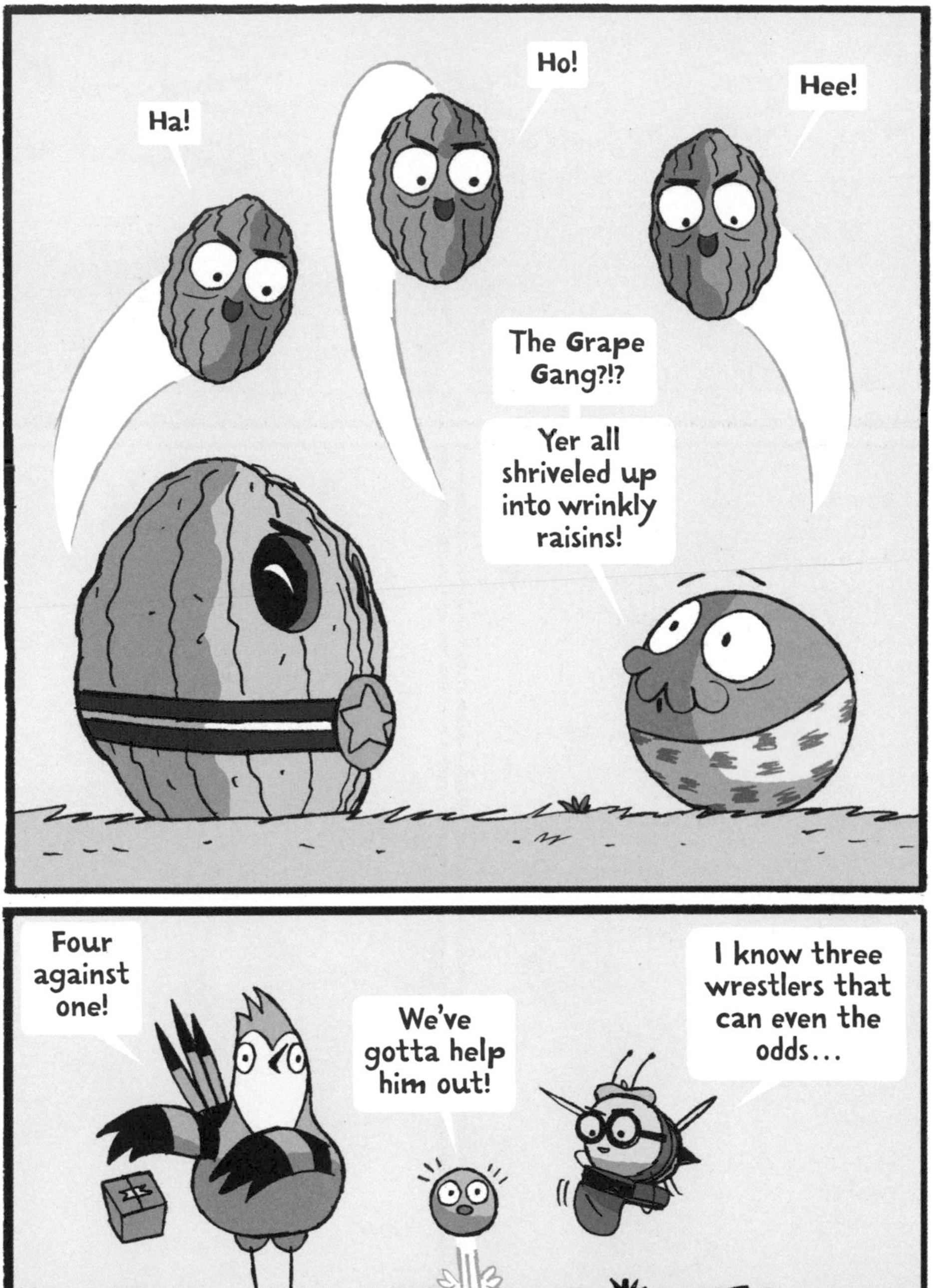
Ha!
Ho!
Hee!
The Grape Gang?!?
Yer all shriveled up into wrinkly raisins!
Four against one!
We've gotta help him out!
I know three wrestlers that can even the odds...

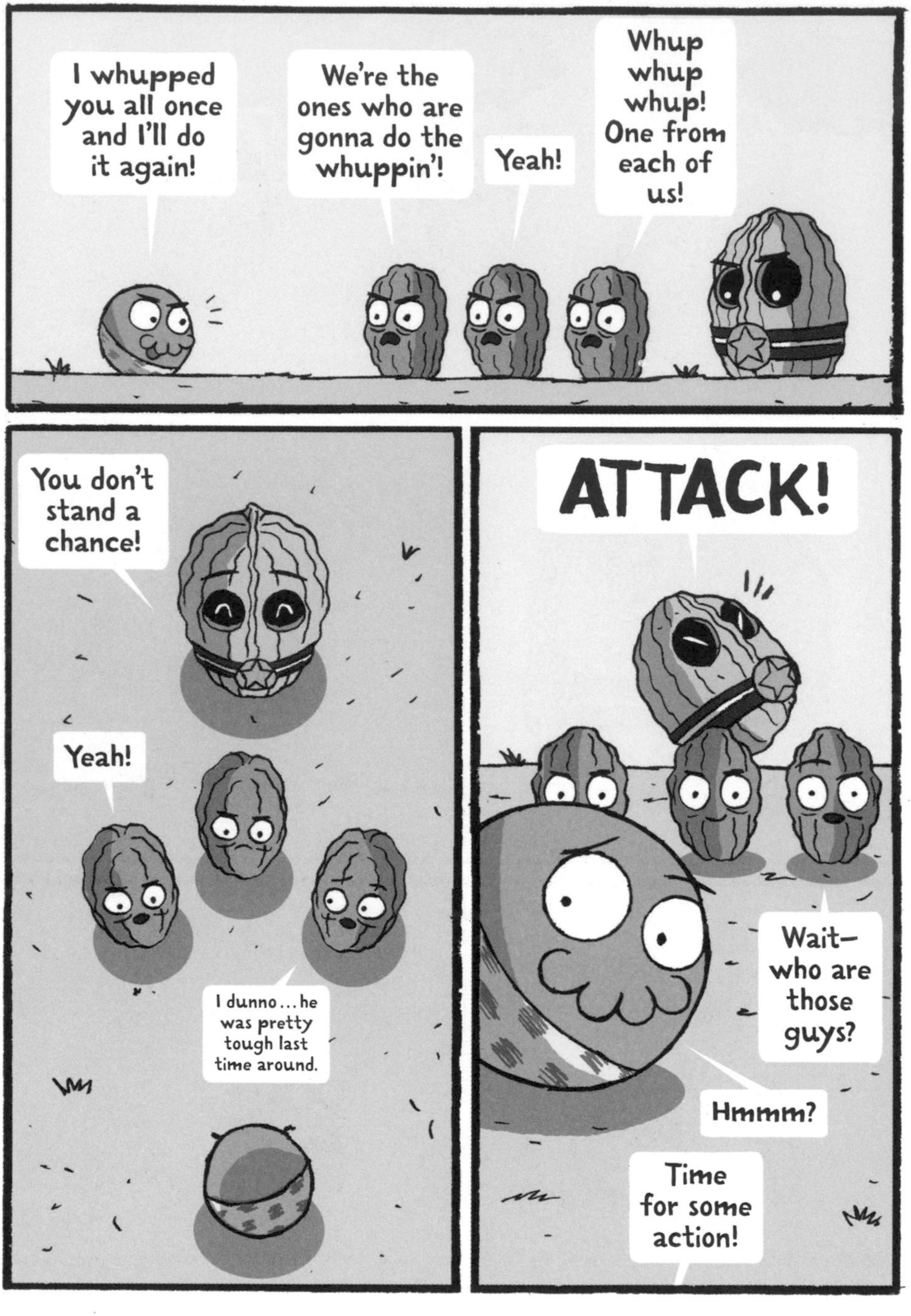
I whupped you all once and I'll do it again!
We're the ones who are gonna do the whuppin'!
Yeah!
Whup whup whup! One from each of us!
You don't stand a chance!
Yeah!
I dunno... he was pretty tough last time around.
ATTACK!
Wait— who are those guys?
Hmmm?
Time for some action!

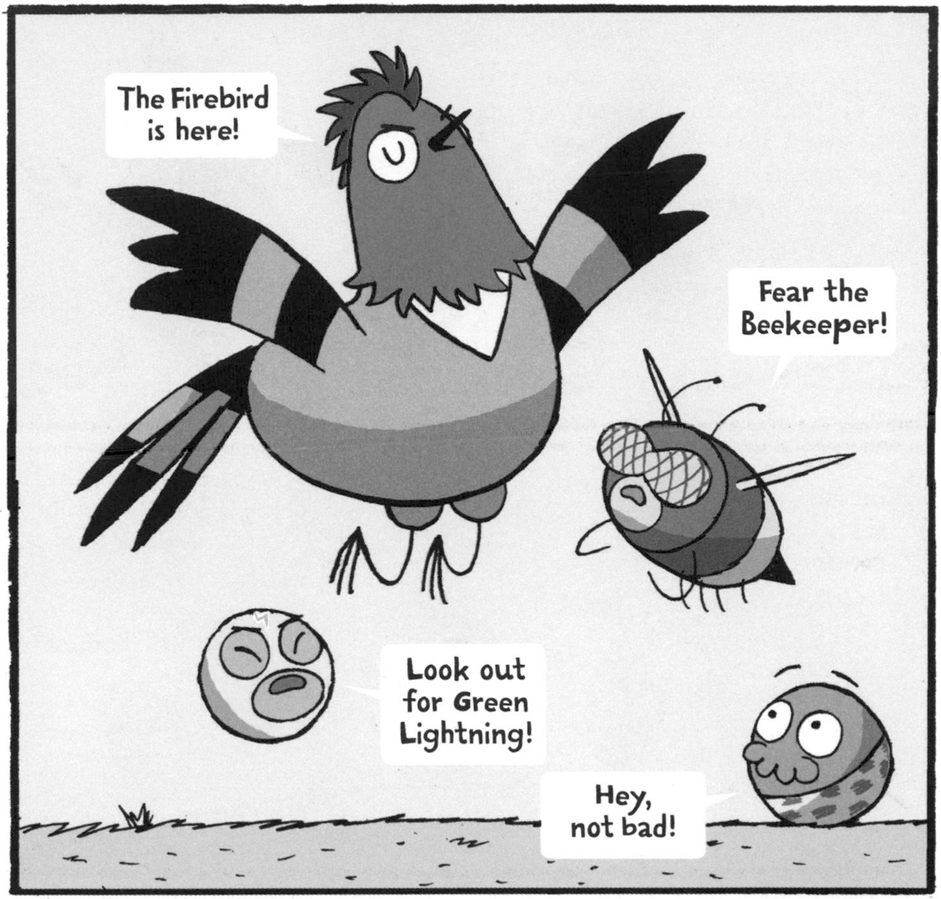
The Firebird is here!
Fear the Beekeeper!
Look out for Green Lightning!
Hey, not bad!

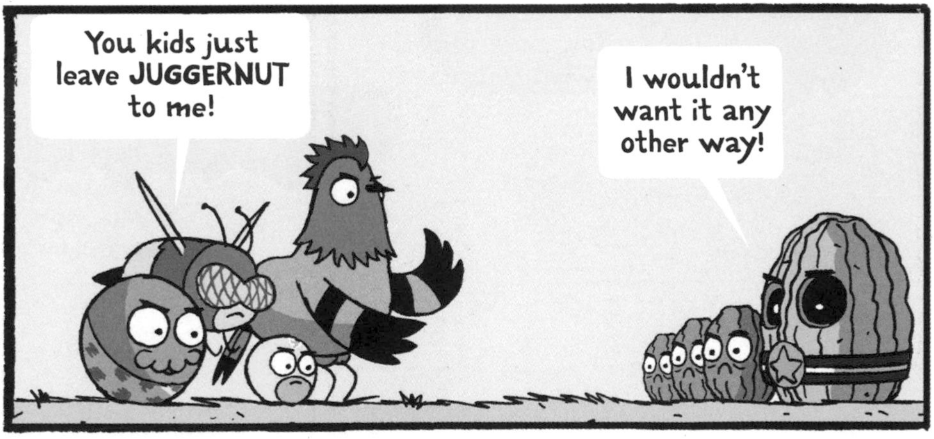
You kids just leave JUGGERNUT to me!
I wouldn't want it any other way!

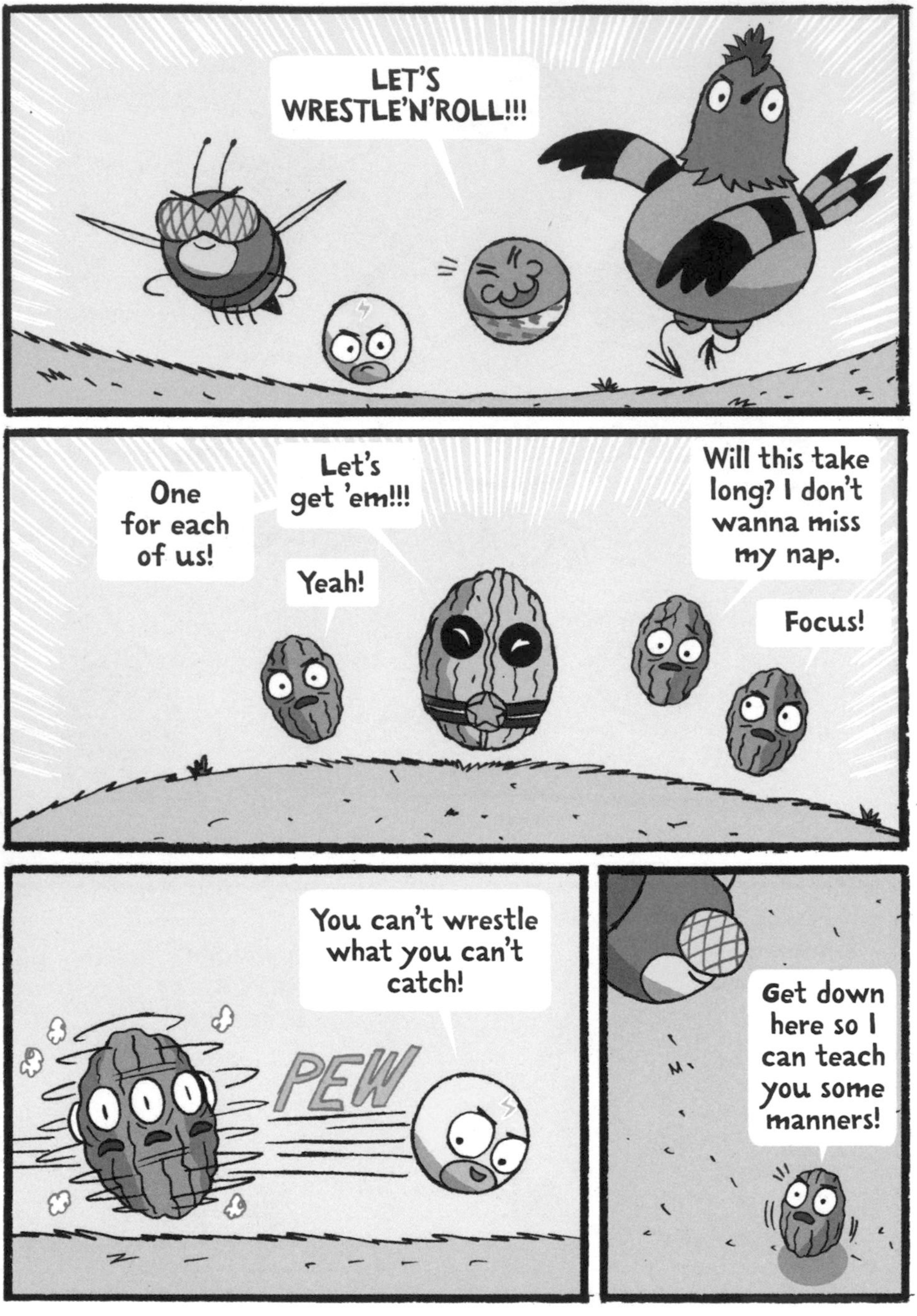
LET'S WRESTLE'N'ROLL!!!
One for each of us!
Let's get 'em!!!
Yeah!
Will this take long? I don't wanna miss my nap.
Focus!
You can't wrestle what you can't catch!
PEW
Get down here so I can teach you some manners!

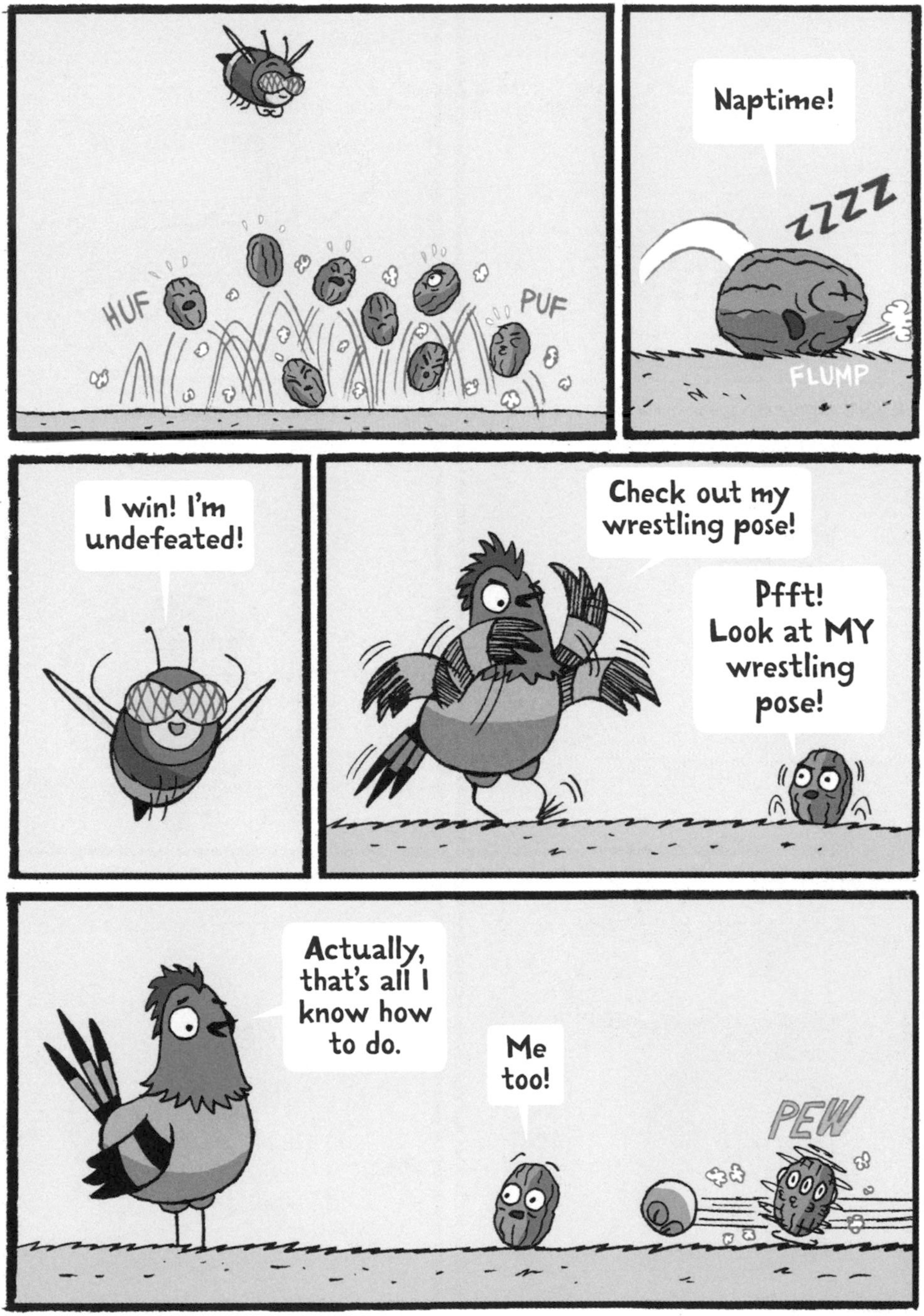
HUF
PUF
Naptime!
ZZZZ
FLUMP
I win! I'm undefeated!
Check out my wrestling pose!
Pfft! Look at MY wrestling pose!
Actually, that's all I know how to do.
Me too!
PEW

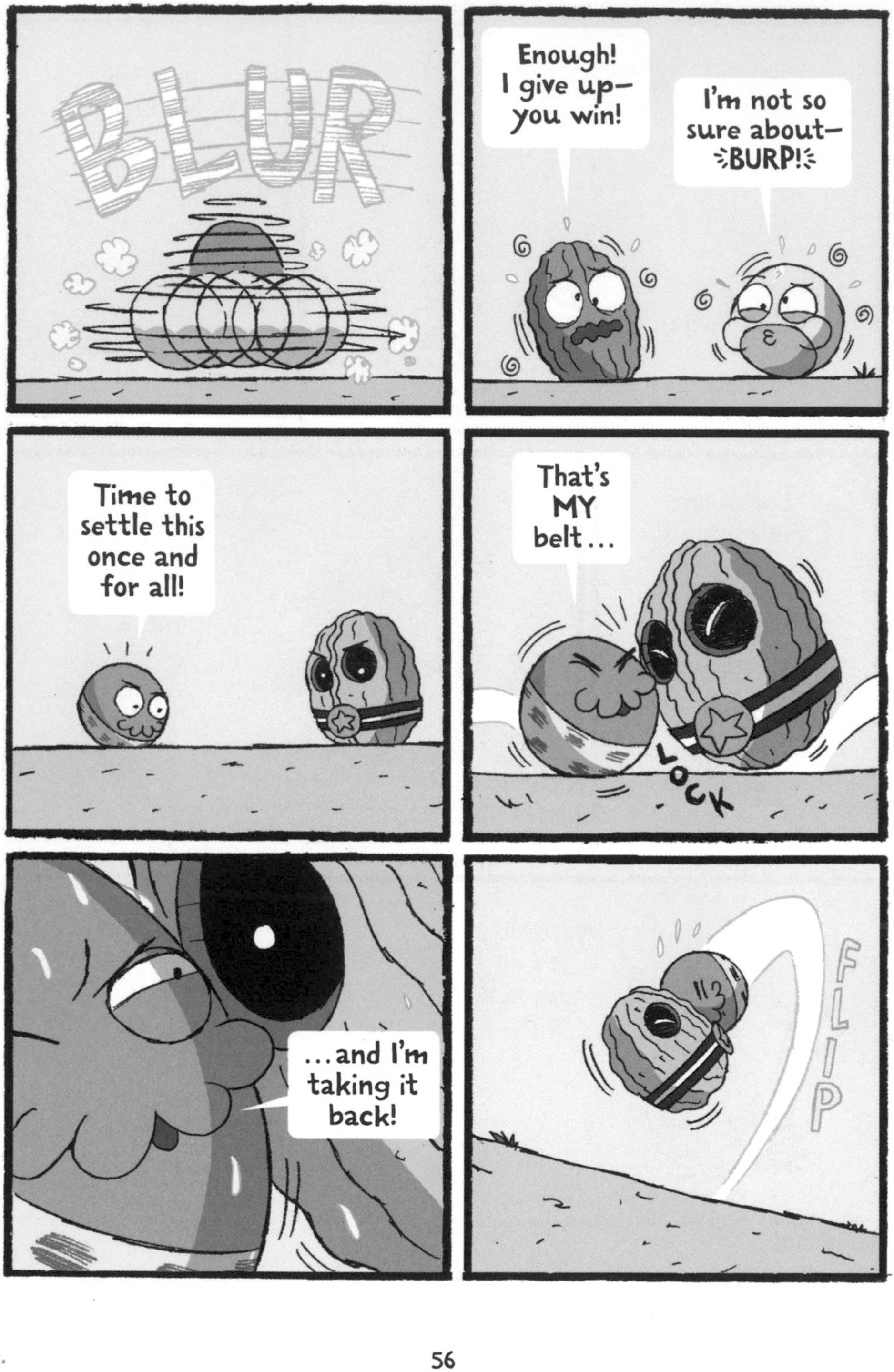
BLUR
Enough! I give up—you win!
I'm not so sure about—BURP!
Time to settle this once and for all!
That's MY belt...
LOCK
...and I'm taking it back!
FLIP

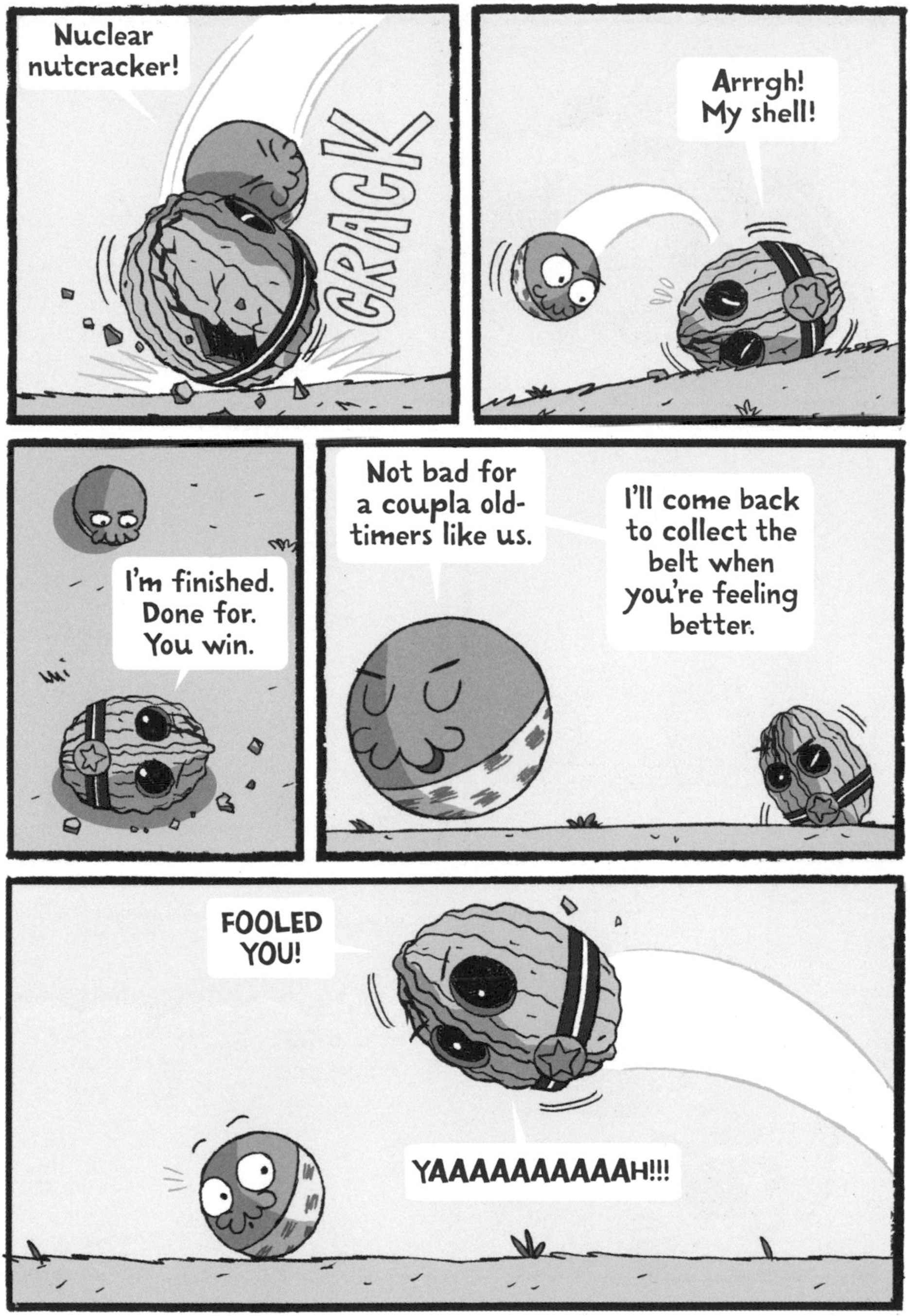
Nuclear nutcracker!
CRACK
Arrrgh! My shell!
I'm finished. Done for. You win.
Not bad for a coupla old-timers like us.
I'll come back to collect the belt when you're feeling better.
FOOLED YOU!
YAAAAAAAAAAH!!!

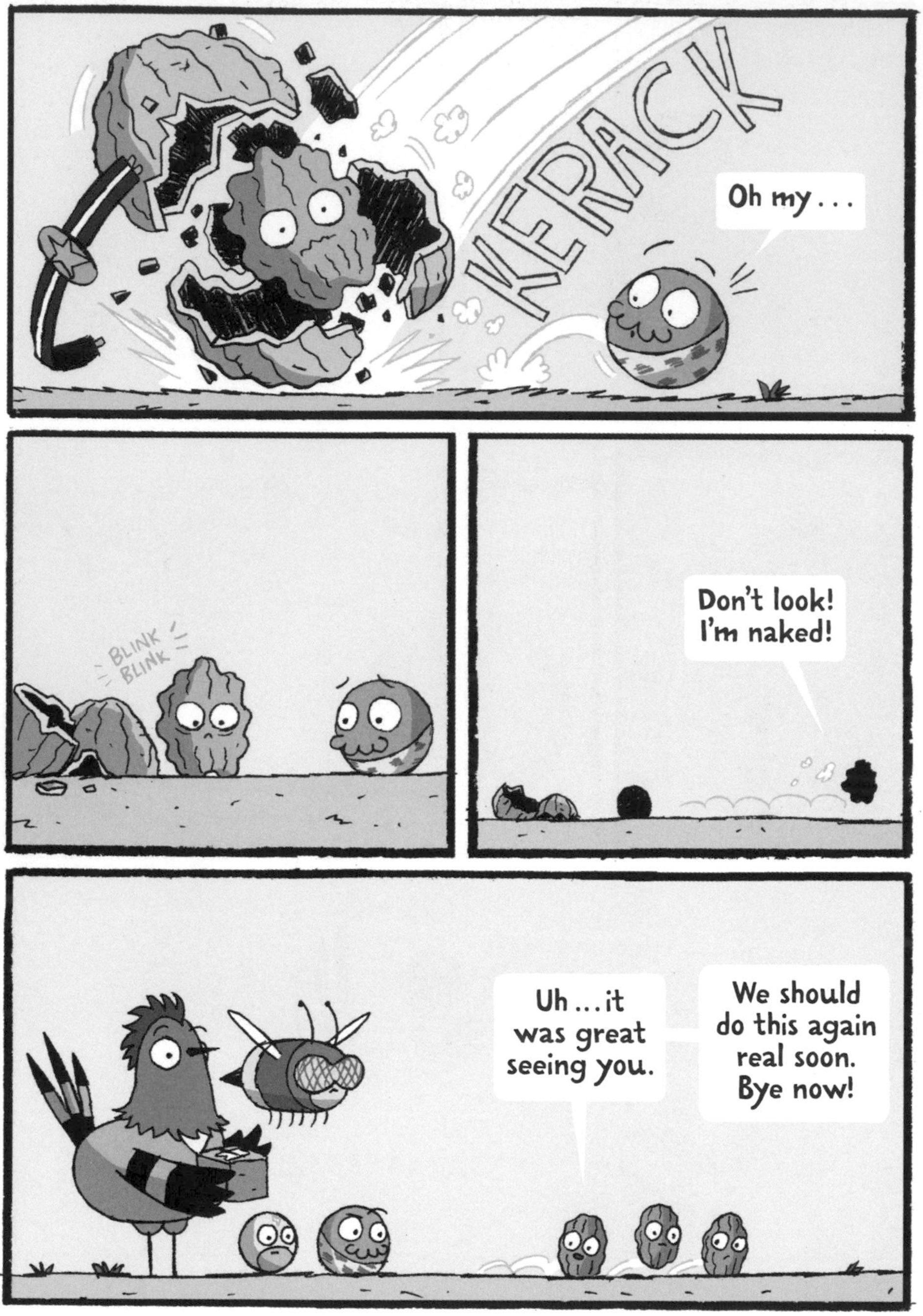
KERACK
Oh my . . .
BLINK BLINK
Don't look! I'm naked!
Uh . . . it was great seeing you.
We should do this again real soon. Bye now!

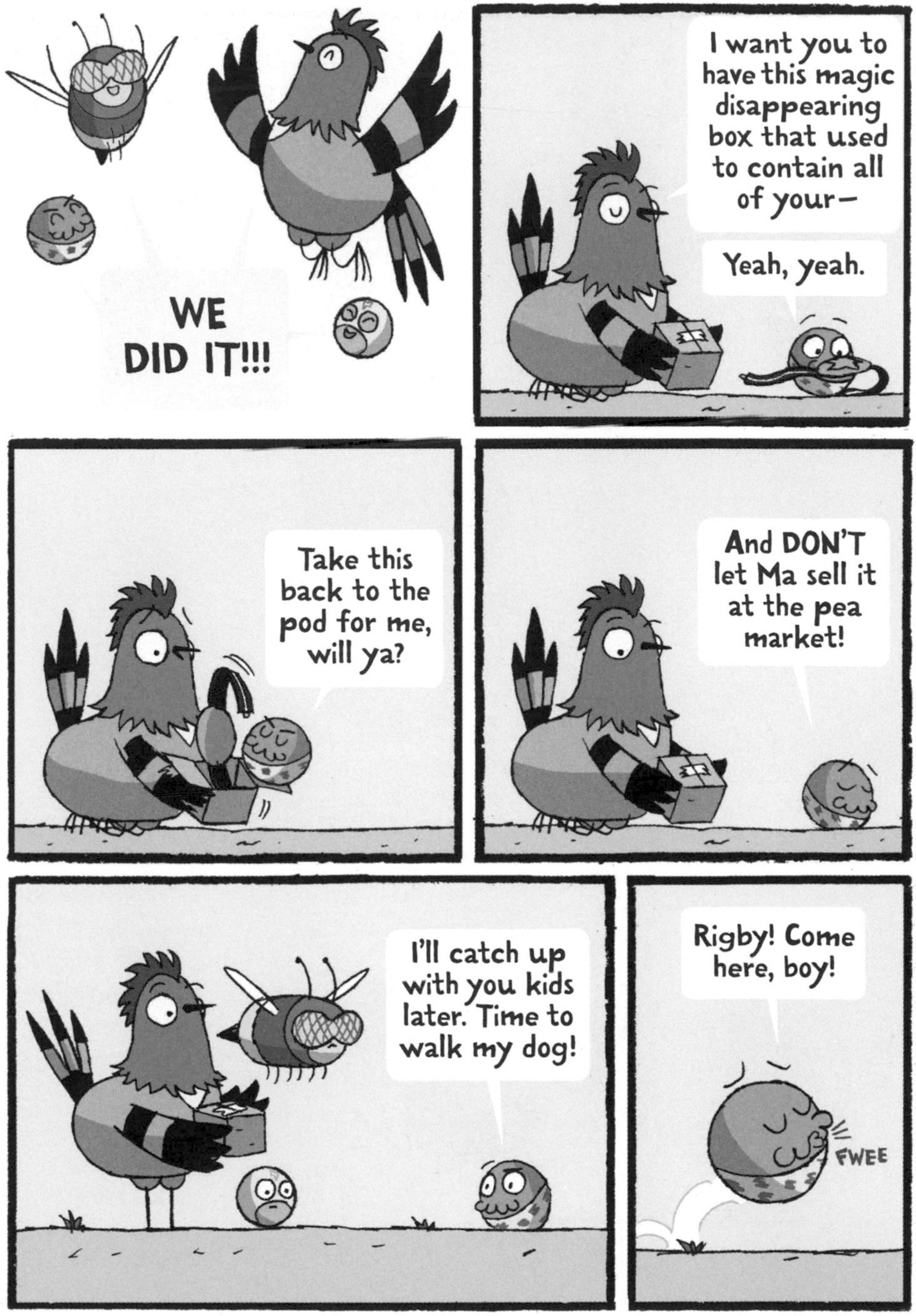
WE DID IT!!!
I want you to have this magic disappearing box that used to contain all of your—
Yeah, yeah.
Take this back to the pod for me, will ya?
And DON'T let Ma sell it at the pea market!
I'll catch up with you kids later. Time to walk my dog!
Rigby! Come here, boy!
FWEE

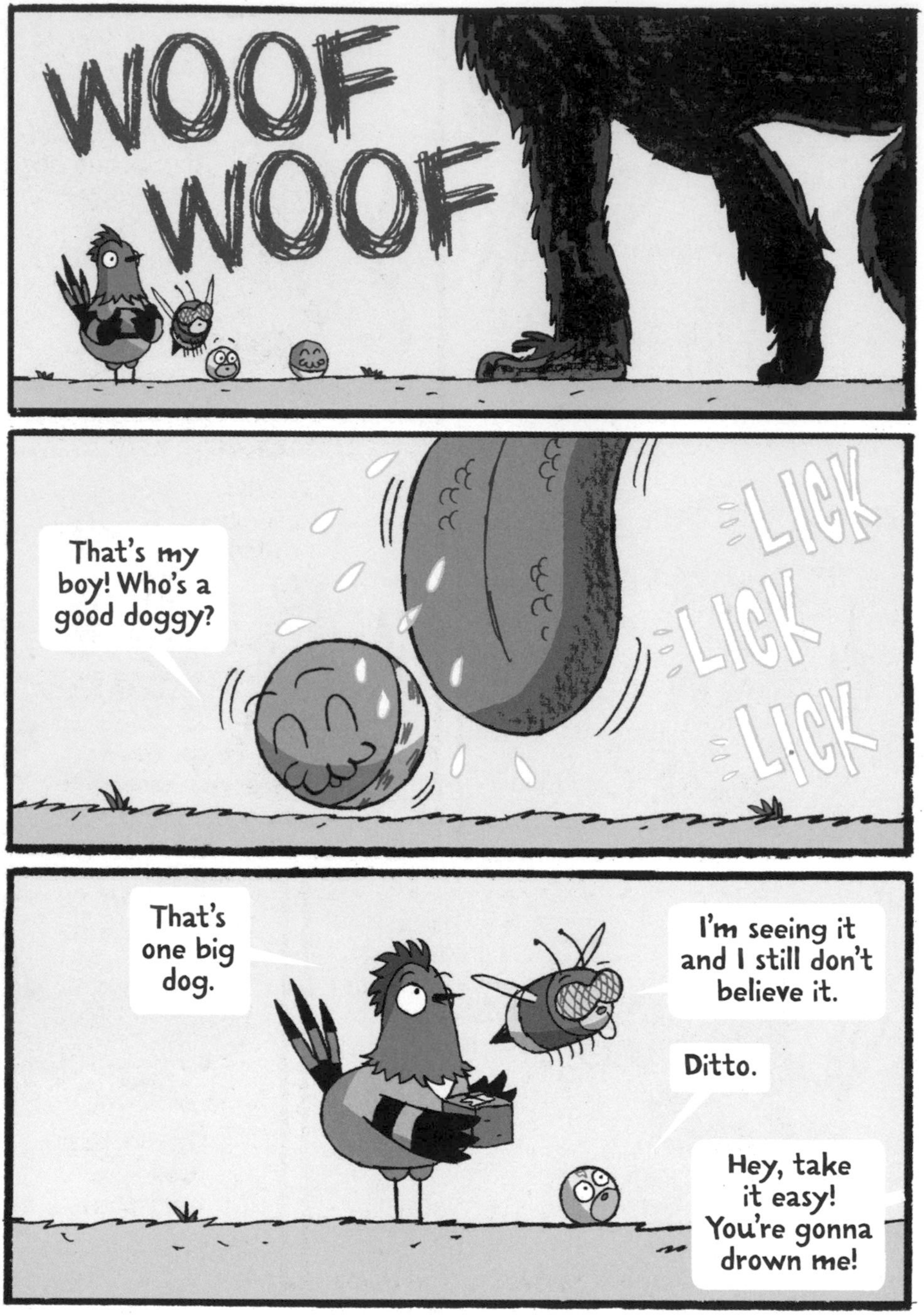
WOOF
WOOF
That's my boy! Who's a good doggy?
LICK
LICK
LICK
That's one big dog.
I'm seeing it and I still don't believe it.
Ditto.
Hey, take it easy! You're gonna drown me!

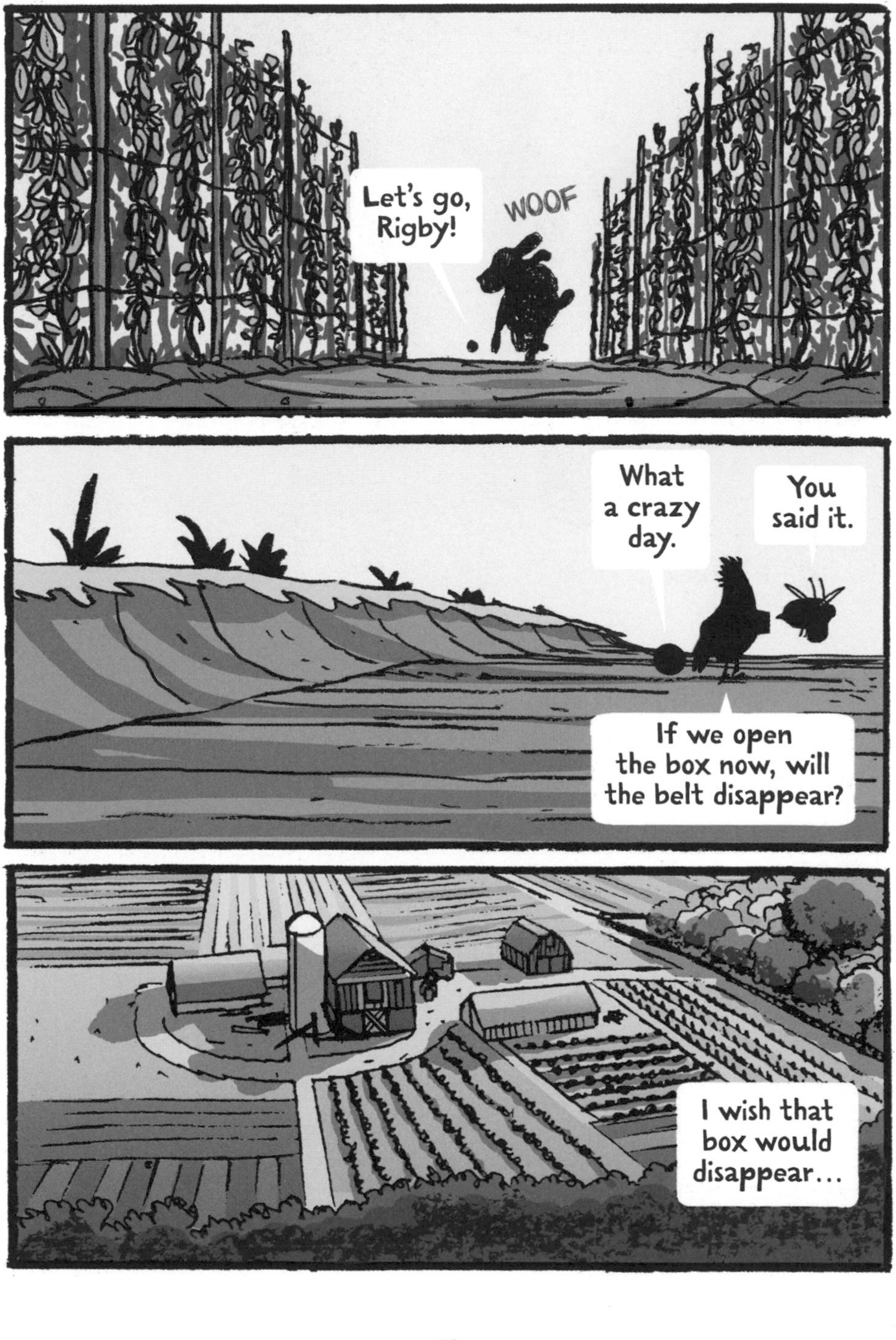
Let's go, Rigby!
WOOF
What a crazy day.
You said it.
If we open the box now, will the belt disappear?
I wish that box would disappear...

Thank you to Bret Parks, Juliet Parks, Elise Parks,
Robin Parks, and Ssalefish Comics, without whom
this book would not have been possible.

HarperAlley is an imprint of HarperCollins Publishers.

Pea, Bee, & Jay #5: Gotta Find Gramps
Copyright © 2022 by Brian Smith
All rights reserved. Manufactured in Italy.
No part of this book may be used or reproduced in any manner whatsoever without written permission
except in the case of brief quotations embodied in critical articles and reviews. For information address
HarperCollins Children's Books, a division of HarperCollins Publishers, 195 Broadway, New York, NY 10007.
www.harperalley.com

ISBN 978-0-06-323669-1 — ISBN 978-0-06-323668-4 (pbk.)

The artist used pencils, paper, a computer, and bee poop (lots and lots
of bee poop) to create the digital illustrations for this book.
Typography by Erica De Chavez
22 23 24 25 26   RTLO   10 9 8 7 6 5 4 3 2 1
❖
First Edition